"This isn't as bad at it looks." His hand slid down her arm to her hand.

Her eyes followed the shiver that ran down her arm at his touch, and settled on the place where his strong calloused hand covered hers. Her heart gave another gasp. "Somebody tried to kill me, Cutch. From *your* land. And now you're trying to stop me from calling the sheriff? I don't think so." She jerked her arm away and looked at him with begging eyes, wanting him to explain, wanting him to say something that would make everything right.

But he hadn't been able to do that eight years ago, and she doubted he could do it now. She knew better than to spend even one more second getting any closer to him than she already was.

Books by Rachelle McCalla

Love Inspired Suspense

Survival Instinct
Troubled Waters
Out on a Limb

RACHELLE McCALLA

is a mild-mannered housewife, and the toughest she ever has to get is when she's trying to keep her four kids quiet in church. Though she often gets in over her head, as her characters do, and has to find a way out, her adventures have more to do with sorting out the carpool and providing food for the potluck. She's never been arrested, gotten in a fistfight or been shot at. And she'd like to keep it that way! For recipes, fun background notes on the places and characters in this book and more information on forthcoming titles, visit www.rachellemccalla.com.

OUT ON A LIMB

RACHELLE McCALLA

Steeple
Hill®

Published by Steeple Hill Books™

STEEPLE HILL BOOKS

Steeple
Hill®

Recycling programs
for this product may
not exist in your area.

ISBN-13: 978-0-373-44410-6

OUT ON A LIMB

www.SteepleHill.com

Printed in U.S.A.

Love your enemies, do good to those who hate you,
bless those who curse you, pray for those
who mistreat you...Do to others as you
would have them do to you.
—*Luke* 6:27–31

Special thanks to my father, retired City of Norfolk
Police Sergeant Brian M. Richter, and to my
brother-in-law, Page County Sheriff's Deputy
Charles McCalla, for answering all my questions
about ballistics, bail and meth. And thank you for
keeping the places we live safe for all these years.
You make the world a better place every day.

Thank you to all the powered hang glider
enthusiasts and pilots of small aircraft who've taken
the time to post videos and instructional materials
for every conceivable flying procedure on the
Internet. I couldn't have written this book without
your help. You make me feel like I can fly.

Thanks also to all the wonderful people at
Steeple Hill, especially my editor, Emily Rodmell,
for doing such a bang-up job on my books.
I feel so tremendously blessed to work with you all!

ONE

Elise McAlister wouldn't have paid any attention to the sound echoing up from the hills below her if she hadn't felt a sharp sting as something grazed her leg. Even then, putting two and two together took her a moment, because the situation went so far beyond anything she'd experienced flying before—or even heard of anyone experiencing. Nobody would really attempt to shoot down a hang glider, would they?

Pop! There it was again.

A spray of shot punched through the fabric of her right wing. The powered glider listed heavily.

"Lord, help me," Elise began to pray as she looked down, frantically trying to assess her situation. Only moments before, she'd been enjoying her Saturday morning flight, soaring peacefully above the scenic Loess Hills of southwestern Iowa, lost in thought and equally detached from any navigational landmarks. Now she was going down and didn't even know where she was.

Pop!

Elise braced herself for this hit, almost relieved to hear the spray take out her motor instead of what remained of her wings. She could glide without a motor. She couldn't stay aloft without wings.

Her hang glider sagged in the air, and the wind messed with the damaged wing, creating drag. Elise spotted a gravel road in the distance. At the rate she was going, there was no way she'd make it—not with all the treetops she'd have to pass over. She was losing altitude fast enough as it was.

Without the steady purr of the motor behind her, she could hear the wind flapping through the torn fabric of her right wing—and below her, the distinctive chinking of metal on metal as a gunman racked the slide on his shotgun. In her mind's eye, she could picture the empty shell kicking out and falling to the ground as a fresh shell was loaded into place, ready to be shot. Sure, she'd taken her dad's twelve gauge out plenty of times, but she hadn't been shooting at anyone.

A dust cloud rose where the gravel road topped a nearby hill. A vehicle was headed this way. If they saw her go down, maybe they could help her—unless they were with whoever was trying to shoot her down.

Blam!

They were getting closer. Elise heard the shots rattle through the thick canopy of leaves below her before ripping through her Dacron again, this time tearing through her left wing. Grateful she'd at least begun to level out, Elise felt her stomach dip as the glider sank toward the treetops.

The jagged hills lunged up to meet her. Below, she could hear shouting, scrambling noises as her pursuers crashed through the underbrush. The gentle breeze, which had clocked in at a pristine six miles per hour when she'd checked it that morning, stilled to almost nothing.

The gun cocked again.

"Please, God, *please*," Elise begged, knowing that, as low in the air as she was now, those shots were going to penetrate deeper. If she was hit again, it would do a lot more than sting a little.

Blam!

The shots tore through her wings again, and a couple balls slammed into the soles of her feet. Maybe her heavy steel-toe hiking boots hadn't been such a bad choice for her morning flight, after all. She didn't usually wear them for flying, but—

Whap! Trees leaves slapped her toes as she skirted the top of a high hill, causing her body to tilt and her wounded craft to tip unsteadily in the air.

Not good. The drag on her wings increased, sapping her momentum, pulling her down. With her pursuers clambering up the hill behind her, she didn't dare go down in this valley. She'd be a sitting duck. They'd be on her before she ever got unstrapped from her harness.

"Lord, I really need your help now," she whispered, her shoulders tensing as she tried to angle upward for maximum lift. She had nothing. No wind. No updraft. She was going down in this valley, and she could hear the gunmen crashing through the woods on the backside of the hill behind her. They'd be on her in a moment.

The next hill careened toward her, its tree-covered sides a mess of fingerlike branches, ready to grab her out of the air and hold her captive until the gunmen caught up to her. Praying hard, she tried to guide her damaged wings upward.

The trees moved closer. She could see each branch. She could see each leaf. She braced herself.

The updraft hit her face at the same second it caught her wings, lifting her clear from the hilltop. "Thank you, God," she prayed, almost-sobbing, instinctively running through the air as the treetops slapped her feet. Though she knew sudden thermal updrafts often occurred on hillsides,

between the timing and her desperation, she felt as though
God had reached down from heaven and pulled her up the
side of the hill just in time.

A dead branch jutted into the sky, and for a moment she
was sure she'd hit it straight on. Lifting her legs, she pulled
up her whole body, bracing herself against her speed bar.
The sole of her boot made contact with the branch, and
she pushed off, effectively propelling herself another ten
feet through the air.

After clearing the trees on the hilltop, her wounded
glider seemed to crumple right out of the sky as the updraft
that had filled her wings dissipated. At least with one more
hillside between her and the gunmen, she'd have some
chance of escaping, however small.

She went down in the treetops of the next valley in
a tangle, her lines, wires and splayed-open fabric wrap-
ping in branches, squeezing her in an unfriendly embrace.
She struggled to unhook her harness, but it wouldn't even
budge against the overwhelming tension as she dangled
from the snarled mess in the treetop.

Elise slapped the side pocket of her parachute pants.
Yes, she'd dutifully remembered to bring her hook knife,
though she'd never had to use it before. Now she whipped
it out and slashed through the nylon restraints, not even
regretting destroying the expensive equipment—not if it
meant saving her life.

With one arm tightly gripping the wedged speed bar,
she tossed the knife uphill where it would be out of her
way, looked down and said another quick prayer before
dropping the last ten feet to the ground. The soft soil of
the Loess Hills felt hard enough when she hit it, meeting
the earth with as much of a roll as she could muster, and
half sliding, half running down the rest of the hill. She

could hear her pursuers shouting as they crashed through the valley behind the hill she'd just crossed over.

She didn't have much time.

Ducking to avoid the jutting branches that jabbed at her from all sides, Elise ran the length of the valley, hoping to skirt the hill and save herself the effort of climbing up the steep, rugged hillside, while at the same time, hopefully, losing her pursuers in the undergrowth.

She ran blindly, fear pushing her as she leaped over fallen logs, swung around saplings and tried to pick her way as quickly as possible over the uneven ground. It would never do to turn an ankle now.

At the side of the hill, the evenly spaced trees gave way to thick bushes, and their sharp briars snagged her as she ran headlong into their midst. About to recoil, she nearly missed seeing the aging fence line that ran through the windbreak. Windbreaks and fence lines didn't just occur randomly. They followed property lines, which usually followed roads.

Elise remembered the road she'd seen from the air. Had she really made it that far? Or would forcing herself into the thick bushes only trap her for the pursuers she could hear topping the last hill behind her?

She threw one arm up in front of her face before ducking headfirst into the briars.

The thorns grabbed relentlessly at her windsuit, tearing through her clothes and snagging her skin. She made it to the barbed-wire fence in one lunge and grabbed the line between the barbs, grateful when it sagged enough to permit her to scramble over. A barb tore at her pants, but she was beyond caring. She could hear the gunmen closing in behind her as she tried to press forward through the unrelenting bramble. She was stuck.

Terror filled her, reminiscent of the nightmares in

which she tried to run but couldn't and awoke to find herself tangled in her bedsheets. But this was no dream. She was stuck in the bushes, and the bad guys were closing in.

Twisting, turning, pushing, she snapped through branches with desperate force, her eyes stinging with tears as thorns bit through her arms and stiff sticks jabbed her ribs. "Please, God. You didn't bring me this far to let me down now."

Scrambling frantically forward, she fell free of the trees and stumbled out onto the chalky, white gravel road.

Right into the path of an oncoming truck.

Brakes squealed as the vehicle threw up a cloud of dust that powdered her face in the same dirty white as the road. Her outstretched hands slapped against the warm hood as the truck's brakes locked, and it slid another couple feet on the loose gravel, roaring to a stop nose-to nose with her. The instant it came to a stop, she ran around to the passenger side of the vehicle, peeling off her flying goggles as the dust began to settle.

The passenger door opened just as Elise recognized the shade of indigo-blue paint underneath the dust-covered sides of the older Dodge Ram. For a second, she thought about diving back into the bushes.

"Need a lift?"

"No," Elise answered instinctively. No way was she getting into a truck with Henry McCutcheon IV. McCutcheons were trouble, and Cutch was the worst kind of trouble. He'd broken her heart eight years ago, and she'd never fully recovered. She certainly didn't need a run-in with him today. His blue eyes twinkled at her from underneath a shock of thick black hair as he leaned across the front seat to address her.

"Elise?" Recognition crossed his perfect features. "Were you flying that glider that just crashed?"

"Uh—"

Before she could fully answer, another gunshot rang through the woods, spitting gravel and shot around her feet and peppering the sides of the truck.

Cutch's blue eyes widened. "Get in!" he shouted.

Elise dived into the cab, pulling the door shut after her as Cutch took off in a cloud of flying gravel. She ducked down as another shot rang out behind them.

"Is somebody shooting at you?" Cutch asked as he gunned the engine, quickly shifting gears as he accelerated.

"Yes," Elise admitted, keeping her head low and wishing her flying helmet was insulated with more than a shock-absorbing layer of Styrofoam. It wasn't made to block a bullet.

"Why?"

"I don't know." Her trembling fingers fumbled with the seatbelt as she attempted to strap herself in. She'd had just about enough after what was supposed to have been a peaceful morning flight through the hills. Her panting stilled as she began to catch her breath.

Cutch quickly put a few more hills between them and their pursuers. "Those guys on foot?" he asked.

"I think so."

"Anybody else after you?"

"I don't know."

The truck slowed as they reached the top of Rink's Mound, the highest hill in the area. Cutch pulled into the parking area near the Loess Hills scenic viewing tower and the old Dodge rumbled to a stop.

It wasn't until the truck had completely stopped moving that Elise realized she was shaking.

Cutch killed the engine and looked over at her.

She shrank against the door and pinched her eyes shut. It was one thing to be shot out of the clear blue sky. It was another thing entirely to be sitting in a truck with Henry McCutcheon IV. Elise wasn't sure which was worse, exactly, but she sure wished she could stop trembling long enough to get the truck door open. They'd dated for a couple of months eight years ago, and he'd only kissed her once, but ever since he'd purposely humiliated her in front of half of Holyoake, she'd steered plenty clear of him.

"Hey." Cutch reached toward her.

She instantly recoiled. "Stay back," she snapped.

He slumped against his seat. "You're the one who jumped into my truck."

"I wouldn't have if there hadn't been somebody shooting at me."

"You're welcome," he said with sarcasm cutting through his voice. "Who was shooting at you, and why?"

"I told you I don't know."

"They shot you out of the sky?" Cutch clarified.

Elise nodded, her shoulders sagging forward as the rush of fear she'd felt was replaced with exhaustion. She pinched the clasp on her chin strap and let her helmet sink into her hands. Then she ran her fingers back through her short, cropped hair, freeing her loose brown curls before tucking the ends behind her ears with trembling fingers.

"That doesn't make any sense. Why would somebody shoot you out of the sky?"

"I don't know." She sucked in a deep breath and tried to think. Why *would* somebody shoot her out of the sky?

"Do you think it was some teenagers playing around?"

"They acted pretty serious." Elise inspected the scratches on her hands and arms from her tangle with the thorn bushes. Drying blood wept from the more serious cuts, but that was the worst of it. She stuck a finger through the hole in her pants where she'd been shot and fingered the spot on her calf where the steel ball had grazed her. It had already stopped bleeding.

Thoughtfully, she prodded the fabric where it gathered at the elastic band near her ankle and felt a ball hiding inside. She leaned down, cautiously peeled back the cuff of her pants and plucked it out.

"What were they shooting?" Cutch continued questioning her. "Birdshot? Do you think they were trying to scare you or something?"

Elise held up the hard metal ball. "Not birdshot. Buckshot," she held the steel ball—over a half centimeter in diameter—in the palm of her hand so he could see. Shot that size was meant to deeply penetrate flesh. "They weren't trying to scare me. They were trying to kill me."

Cutch looked into the warm brown eyes of the woman he'd once loved, and the eight years since their romance seemed to melt away. *Elise.* She was still so attractive, even covered in dust and perched like a frightened bird in the corner of the cab of his truck. So attractive and in spite of the long separation of time, still so familiar to him. What had happened?

"Why would somebody try to kill you?"

"I don't know," she told him again, and he could see from the fear in her eyes that she meant it.

He just couldn't accept it.

"Okay. Help me figure this out. What would you be doing to cause someone to take a shot at you?"

"I was just out flying." Her usually strong voice sounded weak.

"In your powered hang glider?"

She nodded and bit her lower lip.

Cutch felt his heart give an unfamiliar flop. He had no business wanting to pull her into his arms and comfort her, and he had no doubt she'd smack him if he tried it, but he couldn't stop himself from wanting to reach for her. Instead, he gripped the steering wheel, though the truck was parked and the cooling engine tapped out a tune in concert with the grasshoppers whose late-summer songs poured in the open windows.

"So you were out flying in your glider," he prompted.

The woman beside him sniffled, and he watched out of the corner of his eye as she swiped at her cheeks. Elise McAlister was crying in his truck, and somebody had just been trying to shoot her—from his land. He did *not* need this, especially not today.

"Did you see anything unusual before they started shooting?" He risked a glance her way, realizing that if he hadn't gone out early to clear brush on the north quarter, her pursuers would likely have caught up to her. His stomach knotted.

She had her eyes pinched shut, and a trail of wet tears meandered down her dust-cloaked face. "The trees." She sniffled. "The trees are planted in rows back there. And they're all the same. Hickory, I think. Or maybe—"

"Pecan," he supplied reluctantly. It wasn't as though she wouldn't have figured it out on her own, and he needed her to rack her brain for what might have triggered the attack instead of focusing on identifying what kind of trees she'd been flying over.

"Pecan," she repeated in a whisper and looked at him, recognition crossing her features.

She knew. But how much did she know? She didn't know everything, did she? Eight years before, he'd foolishly shared with her his dream of reclaiming his grandfather's pecan groves and clearing the McCutcheon name. And now here he was, already admitting things to her that no one else knew.

Cutch tried to tell himself it didn't matter. What mattered right now was Elise's safety, and he couldn't do anything to help her until he understood what had just happened. "Did you get a good look at the guys who were shooting at you?"

"No. Nothing. They were too far behind me, and the trees blocked my view."

"You ever fly out this way before?"

"Not really. Where were we, exactly?"

"Five miles west of Rink's Mound."

"Do you know who owns that property?"

Cutch returned her gaze, feeling a tiny trickle of relief that she'd regained enough of her composure to ask him such an intelligent question. Of course he knew who owned the property. As the Holyoake County Assessor, he knew down to the last lot and acre who owned what in the whole county. "Yup."

"Who?" An undercurrent of impatience ran through her voice.

He closed his eyes. "Nobody who'd be shooting at you."

"Cutch—" a strangled half panic, half impatience infused itself in her tone "—somebody was trying to kill me. Do you know something?" She glared at him and reached into one of the many zippered pockets on her pants, pulling out a phone. "That's it! Why didn't I think of this sooner? I'm calling the sheriff."

"Wait." He reached out his hand to stop her. The last thing he needed was the sheriff stomping around on his property—especially if somebody was doing something illegal out there. And attempted murder was certainly illegal.

He felt Elise freeze the second his fingers brushed her hand. She looked up at him, and for a moment, time rolled back and they were young again, certain their love could conquer all. They'd been so naive back then.

"Just wait a second. Let's sort this out first." He watched as she swallowed and obediently lowered the phone, though she still held it tightly in her hand.

She repeated her earlier question. "Who owns that property?"

He didn't want to tell her, didn't even want to think about why someone had been shooting at her from his land or what the legal implications might be. But if she was in danger, he couldn't withhold information that might help keep her safe. He met her eyes.

"I do."

TWO

Elise stared at Cutch, the old feelings he stirred up making her heart flop around like a glider caught in a gale. She needed a steady head to sort out what was going on. Having Cutch so close only made things worse.

"*You* own the land from which someone was shooting at me?" she clarified.

He looked back out the window as though he could still see the spot, though it now lay five miles behind them. Meeting her eyes again, he nodded. "Yup."

"That settles it." Elise jerked the door open and slid out of the truck, flicked her phone open and dialed 911. The McCutcheons and the McAlisters had been rivals for generations, even before the McCutcheons had sabotaged her grandfather's plane long before she was born, though it wasn't until his fiery death that the feud had become so fierce. It had been eight years since she'd experienced their direct hostility, and she hadn't thought they'd be so territorial, but she'd always been wrong when she'd dared to trust a McCutcheon in the past. She needed to wise up.

Cutch was out of the truck and around to her side before she could hit Send. "Hang on just a second. This isn't as bad at it looks." His hand slid down her arm to her fingers.

Her eyes followed the shiver that ran down her arm at his touch and settled on the place where his strong, calloused hand covered hers. Her heart gave another dying gasp. "Somebody tried to kill me, Cutch. From *your* land. And now you're trying to stop me from calling the sheriff? I don't think so." She jerked her hand away and looked at him with begging eyes, wanting him to explain, wanting him to say something that would make everything right. But he hadn't been able to do that eight years ago, and she doubted he could do it now. She knew better than to spend even one more second getting any closer to him than she already was.

"Fine." He took a step back and shoved his hands deep into his pockets. "Go ahead and call the sheriff, but where are you going to have him meet you? Here? Or at the scene of the crime?"

"At the scene of the crime."

"And where is that?" Cutch challenged.

"Where I was being shot at. Where my glider went down."

"Yeah? Where'd your glider go down?"

"In your stupid, old pecan grove," she snapped, clicking her phone shut and shoving it back into her pocket. She hated to admit it, but Cutch had a point. She couldn't explain to him where the incident had happened, and he knew the land better than anyone. Before she could direct the sheriff to the spot, she'd need to find out a little more information.

Cutch continued. "My stupid, old pecan grove happens to cover over six-hundred acres. And you can't see something stuck in the trees from one tree to the next, let alone one acre to the next. I'd love to catch whoever was shooting at you, but I doubt they're going to stick around and wave their hands in the air for us to find them. So if you want to direct the sheriff to a crime scene, maybe you ought to figure out where that is first. 'Cause he's a busy man, and I doubt he'll want to tromp around in the woods all day."

"Fine." Elise stomped across the cut-grass parking area toward the lookout tower. "Let's see what we can see from here."

She climbed the sturdy wooden steps with Cutch right behind her, furious with how self-conscious he made her feel. In the eight years since their ill-fated relationship, she'd managed to avoid him almost completely, though that was tough to do in a county of fewer than ten-thousand people.

Once, a few years ago, he'd shown up at one of her glider tutorials at the Holyoake County Fair, and she'd taught him the basics of power gliding in front of a crowd of people. He was clearly a natural at flying and had performed well, but she'd ended up going home that night and crying into her pillow. That was the kind of effect he had on her. And she didn't need that kind of complication when she was trying to sort out who'd shot down her glider.

Elise reached the top of the scenic tower and leaned on the western rail. The land spread out before her in a jagged, tree-covered expanse, the hills jutting up at steep angles, the valleys dipping down in deep shadows. The Loess Hills were beautiful in their own way, though the sandy soil and harsh terrain made farming them all-but-impossible. Everyone who'd tried to make a living off the hills had ended up impoverished. They were nice to look at—that was all.

A haze of late-summer heat made the air shimmer on

the horizon. "Where's your pecan grove?" she asked as Cutch joined her by the rail.

"My *stupid, old* pecan grove?" His icy-blue eyes swept over her, chilling her. "It's over there."

Elise tried to look where he pointed. Trees. Trees. More trees. Hills with trees on them and more trees. Nothing that screamed *pecan grove*.

"Where?" she asked impatiently.

His arm extended, his finger still pointing westward, Cutch stepped closer to her, his body fitting neatly against hers like a bird tucking its young under its wing. A warm rush flooded through her as he settled his other hand on her shoulder and aligned his face with hers.

"See where I'm pointing?" His gentle breath joined the breeze as it cooled her cheek.

"Uh-huh." Elise could see nothing. She was aware of Cutch and his closeness and how much she wanted to just let those strong arms wrap around her and hold her after the scare she'd had in the air. But thoughts like that would only get her into trouble. Cutch had sweet-talked his way into her heart before, though he'd only done it to make a fool out of her. She could do without a repeat of that lesson. She blinked and tried to focus. "Do you see anything?" She licked her lips and tried to restore some moisture to her mouth, but her throat had gone completely dry.

"Pecan trees."

Elise sighed. "No sign of my glider?"

"Nope. Just trees." Cutch stepped away from her and lowered his hand to the wooden railing.

Finally able to breathe again, Elise kept her eyes on the distant trees, not trusting herself to look at him while she spoke. "I think I should call the sheriff. Even if we don't know exactly where my glider went down, and even if those guys are long gone, I'll feel a lot better once I report what happened." Or at least she hoped she'd feel better.

She turned and saw the hesitation in his eyes, and when he first opened his mouth, she thought for sure a protest was on his lips. Instead, he worked his face into a grimace and pinched his eyes shut. "Fine. Call the sheriff. I'll do whatever I can to cooperate with an investigation."

Though his obvious struggle made her curious, Elise didn't give Cutch an opportunity to change his mind. She pulled her phone back out and started to dial.

"I'm going back down," Cutch said quietly, then turned and headed for the stairs.

"Wait," she called after him, her finger hesitating over the Send button. "You're not going to leave me out here all alone, are you?" She didn't know who had been shooting at her or where they were now. The last thing she wanted was to be left alone where they might catch up to her.

"Of course not. I just thought you might appreciate some privacy. I'll wait on the ground for you to finish your call." He looked slightly injured that she might have thought he'd abandon her.

Elise felt chastised and realized she was infringing on his time. "You don't have somewhere else you need to be?"

"Nothing so important that I'd leave you out here."

The look in his eyes addled her brain. She couldn't decide if he looked resentful or hurt or honestly as though he cared about her. Though she knew that last one *couldn't* be it, she couldn't deny the gentle compassion that fueled his words. Not willing to think about why he'd speak to her like that, she pressed Send and held the phone to her ear.

Cutch headed down the stairs of the lookout tower, and Elise watched him go, her heart still hammering hard, though the fear and the long run through the woods was now twenty minutes or more behind her. No, she was pretty sure the reason her heart was hammering was Henry McCutcheon IV.

Cutch slowly walked to his truck, listening to the sound of Elise's voice over the birdsong in the woods around them. He couldn't clearly make out any of her words any more than he could sort out how his morning had taken such an about-face turn in one startled moment.

When he'd headed out to clear trees that morning, he'd promised his mother he'd be back to the house in time for his dad's exam. That was the whole reason they'd scheduled it for a Saturday—so he could be there. The home-visit nurse was set to arrive in less than ten minutes. There was absolutely no way he could make it there in time—not unless he abandoned Elise. He pulled out his phone and called his mother, letting her know he'd stopped to help a friend and wouldn't be back in time for the appointment.

As much as Cutch wanted to be there to support his parents through the most difficult parts of his father's hospice treatment, he knew ultimately there wasn't any tangible reason for him to be there. No matter what he did, his father was going to die. He'd accepted the inevitable, though it tore at him.

After placing the call, Cutch shoved his phone back into his pocket and leaned on the truck. On the lookout tower above him, he could still hear Elise talking. He closed his eyes and listened to the feminine cadence of her voice carrying on the late summer breeze.

Elise. Falling in love with her eight years before had been too easy. Getting over her—well, the only way he'd figured out to cope with that was to pretend she didn't exist. He'd long ago given up trying to sort out a way to make a relationship between them work. McCutcheons and McAlisters were destined to hate each other. He'd endured enough heartache the last time he'd tried to defy that truth.

Though he tried to cut off his feelings toward her, his heart squeezed thinking about how frightened she'd been when she'd jumped into his truck. Who would have been on his property that morning? No one was supposed to have been out there, certainly not with a gun. He had No Trespassing and No Hunting signs posted all around the property's perimeter. His land was a tranquil retreat—not a place for a young woman to be shot out of the sky and left running for her life.

Could it have been an accident? From what he'd seen of her crash from his truck, she'd gone down pretty fast. In fact, he'd slowed down and been watching the woods when she'd burst out of the bushes in front of him. Though he didn't know of anyone else in Holyoake County who owned a powered hang glider, he was still shocked to see her frightened face when he'd opened the door of his truck.

But why would someone want to hurt Elise? Other than the McCutcheons, who'd held a grudge against the McAlisters for far too long in his opinion, there wasn't anyone in town who didn't like Elise—at least not that he knew of. She was a sweet, spunky girl whose soft side showed through a little more than she'd like. He smiled just thinking about her.

At the sound of footsteps, Cutch looked up and watched Elise trotting lightly down the steps. She appeared to be in better spirits and certainly looked less shaken. Relief coursed through him. He hadn't liked seeing her so distraught.

"Did you get in touch with the sheriff?" he asked.

"Yes." She offered him a smile. "I spoke with Sheriff Bromley. He agreed there probably wasn't much sense in him driving out here when we don't have a crime scene for him to look at. But he took down all the details I could remember."

"And you're all right with that?" Cutch pressed.

Elise looked sheepish. "I guess I feel a little silly asking him to come out here and poke around when there probably isn't much for him to find."

"But if someone tried to kill you—"

"We don't know for a fact that's what they were doing."

"That's not the conclusion you reached earlier."

"I'm calmer now that I've talked with Sheriff Bromley. He didn't sound too concerned—"

"He didn't sound concerned?" Cutch had to interrupt. Elise's safety was important, even if she didn't think so.

"Well, of course he was concerned for *me*. But he didn't figure there would still be any threat now that I got away safely. Probably just some teenagers goofing around." She shrugged.

"Teenagers? Goofing around by shooting buckshot at a person? The teenagers I know are all smarter than that." Cutch didn't want to upset her, but he'd rather have her upset than dead. And if she underestimated the threat against her, well, he didn't want to consider what could happen.

Elise glared at him. "Whatever. You should be glad I'm not pressing charges against you."

"Charges for what? Picking you up before the gunmen caught up to you?"

"No. Because I was being shot at from your land."

Her nostrils flared as she glared at him. "I need to call someone to come pick me up."

"No, you don't. I can give you a ride. Where are you headed?" He didn't like the way she accused him, then dismissed him. Did she really not trust him at all?

"The airfield. But that's really not necessary."

"It's no problem," he insisted, rounding the truck to the driver's seat.

She didn't budge from where she stood in front of his truck. Her lips twitched, but she didn't speak.

He met her eyes. Why did she have to be so stubborn, anyway? "Elise?"

She looked from him to the passenger seat and back again. "I don't know."

Folding his hands over the hood of the truck, he leaned on his arms and looked at her. "Why not? You need a ride, and the airfield is on my way. It's no big deal."

"If Uncle Leroy sees me with you—"

Cutch blew out an exasperated breath. He knew the McAlisters didn't like his family, but he couldn't imagine Elise's father's brother getting into that big of a fit. Still, if she was concerned... "I'll hide," he offered.

The little hint of a smile that peeked out at him warmed his heart, though a second later she replaced it with a scowl. "I don't want to keep you from your busy schedule."

Thinking of his father's exam that he'd already missed, he shrugged. "If I say I have time to drop you off, I have time."

Elise took a tentative step toward the passenger side of the truck, then looked back at him. "Thank you," she said quietly.

For a moment the humid air stilled between them, and that simple courtesy seemed to shout so much more. Could *thank you* mean *I still love you?* Or *I'm sorry for the past eight years?* Or even *I wish none of our family's feud had ever come between us?* He thought he heard those words hidden between her simple thanks, but then he'd always been a dreamer. Time to pull his head out of the clouds.

"No problem." Cutch nodded and hopped in the driver's side, relieved when Elise climbed in, too. "So, to the airport," he announced, turning the key. "What are you planning to do when you get there?"

"I'm going to take my Cessna up and fly over your property. I've got a portable GPS unit that I can use to get the exact coordinates of my glider's location. Then I can take the GPS with me to find the spot when I go on foot to retrieve it."

Cutch turned the truck around and headed back out onto the gravel road. "You're planning to retrieve your glider, hmm? Do you have permission from the property owner to be on the land?" The words were meant to be a gentle tease. He hoped they'd elicit a smile.

But instead her pretty face frowned. "You said it was your land."

"That's right. So are you going to ask for my permission, or are you planning to trespass illegally?"

"Cutch," she protested. "I can't believe you're making an issue of this—especially after what I've been through today."

Hurt that she'd taken his words the wrong way, he defended himself, still maintaining the lighthearted undertone he'd begun with, though she obviously hadn't picked up on it. "Yeah, well, I've recently become aware of issues with trespassers on my land. Apparently some of them shot down a hang glider earlier, so I feel like I need to crack down." He glanced over to gauge her reaction.

"You're a couple hours too late to do my glider any good."

Something in the back of his brain screamed *mayday!* He couldn't let her be mad at him—couldn't let her walk out of his life again, not with her angry like this. "Then let me make it up to you. Take me up in your plane, and I'll help you find the spot it went down."

"I don't think so!" she snapped.

"Why not? I know the land better than anyone. I can help you locate your glider more quickly, and I may be able to spot signs of where your gunmen may have been when they shot at you. If we could find an empty casing or footprint, then the sheriff would have something to come out and take a look at."

Elise shook her head forcefully. "I can find my glider myself. Once I get a GPS lock on the location, I can find it from the ground. I don't need your help."

"But you need my permission to be on my land."

"Did the gunmen have your permission?"

They were nearly to the airport by this time, and Cutch felt his hackles rising. What had started out as a hint of teasing had blown way out of proportion, but why was he surprised? Elise still knew how to push his buttons. It was a good reminder of why things hadn't worked out between them eight years ago—why they would never work out. But he still wasn't about to let her fly into danger alone. He'd never forgive himself if she was shot down a second time.

"The gunmen were trespassing—" he let his tone drop to a low, even rate, let the warning carry through in his words "—and if I ever find out who it was, you can believe I'll press charges. Nobody hurts you and gets away with it."

Elise felt a shiver run down her spine at the chilly threat behind Cutch's words. But what made her nearly gasp was the zealous protection implied in his final statement. Didn't he realize how much *he* had hurt her? Just the memory of the way he'd set her up for humiliation eight years before made her heart squeeze and the old wounds cry out in pain. Their first and only kiss, the moment she'd dreamed about since she'd first fallen in love with him, had turned out to be a trick, a stunt he'd pulled to embarrass her in front of half of Holyoake. In fact, their entire relationship had been a farce, another way for a McCutcheon to humiliate a McAlister.

Still, she figured she was mature enough to work with him without letting on to the distress he caused her heart. She'd just have to keep him at arm's length and stomp down any tender feelings, such as those that had flooded her when he'd put his arm around her on the viewing tower. Surely she could handle that…

"I'd like to come with you. I'm sure I can help." Cutch announced matter-of-factly as he parked the truck behind the hangar and killed the engine.

What could she say? He seemed intent on going up with her, and honestly, after the terror she'd felt that morning, it would be an enormous comfort to have along a strong man she could trust. She just wasn't convinced Cutch was that man. But she was in a hurry to find her glider, and he was probably correct about being able to help her quickly locate it in the thick trees. She'd scrambled through the woods in such a blur that little clear memory remained to guide her.

"If I'm not imposing on your time—"

"You're not."

"Then let's hurry. I still don't want Uncle Leroy to see you."

They ducked out of the truck and went around the hangar to the door facing the airfield. "Leroy's probably in the office. He and Rodney are usually the only ones around on Saturdays," Elise explained, opening the wide hangar door. "They shouldn't see us if we use this door."

She hurried over to her Cessna 172 Skyhawk and patted the white-with-red-stripes plane affectionately on one wing. "This is my baby," she informed Cutch.

"Looks like your baby is older than you are."

"She is," Elise admitted, circling the plane as she initiated her preflight check. "But I'm saving my pennies to buy her a little sister. Aren't I, darling?" She gave the rudder a gentle tug. "Anyway, she's a good little bird and keeps me in the sky, which is more than I can say for my powered hang glider."

"You don't think there's a chance somebody will try to shoot this girl down, do you?" Cutch looked concerned.

Elise faced him under the wing. "We should be out of the range of a shotgun. I fly my glider at a lot lower elevation than I fly my plane."

"But when you're dusting crops—"

"That's different." Elise wasn't fond of crop dusting and wished her aerial photography business was self-sustaining enough so she could give up working for her uncle. But so far, her dreams had yet to pan out. "I'm capable of flying low, but I wouldn't try it in those hills. Besides, this plane is a lot faster and way more maneuverable than my glider. I can get out in a hurry at the first sign of trouble."

Cutch seemed to accept her response and stayed quiet as she finished checking the plane and climbed aboard. She reached behind his seat for the extra headset and noticed her camera still in the backseat of the four-seat plane. A thought occurred to her.

"Do you know much about taking pictures?" she asked.

He grinned back slyly. "Don't you recall my 4-H entries?"

Elise almost smiled back, but then she remembered the year he'd swept the purple ribbon right out from under her. She'd been nine years old, he eleven, and though she now realized the composition of his scenic Loess Hills landscape had been precociously perfect, at the time, she'd been devastated. Her father had chalked up the incident to just another example of how she couldn't trust a McCutcheon. "Can you still use a camera?"

"Maybe not as well as you can, but well enough."

She handed him the digital camera and explained. "It's all set for aerial photographs, so all you'll have to do is point and shoot. Oh, and don't erase the stuff on my memory card—I was out with Rodney yesterday taking pictures of the Mitchum's corn maze. I haven't had a chance to download the pictures yet."

Cutch accepted the camera from her. "How's the aerial photography business going?"

Her mind focused on the preflight check, Elise murmured a distracted response. "It keeps me busy, but it doesn't pay the bills. I have to pay a pilot to take me up since it's impossible to fly and take pictures at the same time. That takes a big chunk out of my profit." She toggled a switch. "So I still do crop dusting for Leroy on the side."

"That's too bad. You're such a talented photographer."

Cutch's comment surprised Elise, and she looked up from her checklist to find him leaning across his seat toward her, his face much nearer to hers than she'd have liked inside the close quarters of the cockpit. She felt her cheeks turn red and looked nervously back down at the laminated booklet in her hands. "As I recall, you're the one who won the purple ribbon."

"Only once. You won it every other year."

"But that's the year I remember." When she dared to glance back up at him, she found him still leaning her way, still looking at her in that unsettling way that made her heart leap inside her more violently than it did during a bad landing.

"Funny what we choose to remember," he said, chuckling softly and turning away to adjust the headset over his ears.

Elise pulled her attention back to her preflight checklist. She had to focus. Though she'd been flying for years and knew the drill backward and forward, having Cutch in her plane was just the kind of distraction that could cause her to miss something, and today was the last day she wanted that to happen.

"Sky Belle to Big Bird, Sky Belle to Big Bird." She radioed Uncle Leroy in the office.

"Sky Belle, this is Big Bird. What are you up to this morning?"

Elise relayed their flight plan to her uncle, who okayed her for takeoff. Fortunately, he didn't ask any questions about why she was headed out. If she'd talked to him in person first, he certainly would have done so then, but she knew he liked to keep their radio conversations strictly professional, which was why she'd waited until she was in the plane to talk to him. Hopefully, he wouldn't suspect anything strange was up.

With Cutch safely buckled in, Elise taxied out and lifted off, feeling more in control with her plane in the air than she had since she'd heard the first shot that morning. She was at home in the sky. It was her peaceful retreat where none of the pain in her life—not her absent mother or her struggling business or the ongoing feud with the McCutcheons—could trouble her. The invasion of her peace was just another reason why the attack that morning had disturbed her so deeply.

The airspace of southwestern Iowa was empty as usual, and the clear skies and gentle breeze made for perfect flying conditions. They quickly and uneventfully found themselves closing in on Cutch's pecan grove. Elise aligned the plane with what she could recall of her flight path that morning.

"We're right above where I was flying earlier," she explained to Cutch. "We're coming up on the spot where I heard the first shot."

"When we get to that area, can you try to get a little closer and maybe circle around? I haven't had the opportunity to fly over the property in years, not since my Grandpa McCutcheon used to give me flying lessons, but I'd like to think if there was something out of place I'd be able to spot it from the air."

"Sure," Elise agreed. "There's a pretty wide valley about there where it's almost level for a good stretch. I shouldn't have any trouble coming around." She eased the plane a little lower in the sky. "Seems like I was right around here when I heard the first shot."

Cutch had his face nearly plastered to the window. "Right there," he said with excitement. "I see something below us. Can you come around again?"

"Go ahead and open that window," Elise instructed as she swung the plane in a wide arc. "I've taken the screw out so you can remove the pane and stick your head out. You can even use the camera outside the window. Just make sure you don't drop it."

Elise kept her eyes on where she was headed, focusing on maneuvering between the tree-covered hills, but she heard the air rush in as Cutch successfully removed the Plexiglas window.

"Does that give you a better view?"

"Much better." He started clicking away with the camera before asking, "Is this close to where they started shooting at you?"

"We just passed over the spot. Why?"

Cutch pulled his head in and lowered the camera. "I know why they were shooting at you. And you're probably right—they weren't just trying to spook you. I think they wanted you dead."

THREE

"What?" Elise startled at the controls and had to force herself to pay attention to what she was doing. Her pulse rate kicked up. Though the nature of the attack had indicated malicious intent, she'd been trying to convince herself ever since that the cause was more innocent. She didn't like what the alternative implied. "Are you serious?"

"I wish I could say I was joking. And I really wish I hadn't seen what I just saw." His words sounded somber, strained.

"What was it?" Elise nearly screeched in her fear and impatience.

"I'm almost certain that was an anhydrous ammonia tank down there."

"Anhydrous ammonia? What's so sinister about that?" The white tanks, their sides and ends brightly painted with warnings identifying the volatile contents, were a common site in agrarian Holyoake County. "Farmers use anhydrous all the time on their crops. I see those tanks every day."

"Not in a pecan grove, you don't." Cutch replaced the window, and the air stilled inside the small cabin.

The relative silence felt suddenly oppressive. "I take it the tank doesn't belong to you?"

"Absolutely not." The force behind Cutch's statement

surprised Elise. "I don't know how it got out there or who brought it out there. But unfortunately, I think I know what they're using it for."

Elise recalled reading something about anhydrous in a newspaper article some time back, but she hadn't had a reason to pay much attention then. Now she tried to recall what the article had said. "Something about drugs?" she asked quietly.

"Yes. Drugs." Cutch took a couple of deep breaths. From the corner of her eye, Elise could see his broad chest rise and fall, straining against the shoulder strap of his safety restraint. "I think someone's making metham-phetamine. *On my property.*"

Barely suppressed anger simmered in the air. Elise wished she knew what she could say to comfort him, because he appeared to be quite distraught by his discovery.

Finally she asked the question that had been haunting her. "And that's why they shot at me? They think I saw what they were doing?"

"That would be my guess." Cutch concluded. "And as much as I don't like it, I'd also guess they know who you are. Most of the county is aware you're the only person with a powered hang glider in these parts, just like pretty much everybody knows you're into aerial photography. They might even think you already took a picture of them or were about to before they started shooting."

Elise's stomach plummeted as she dipped the plane back around, heading back out along the path her wounded glider had taken. For the first time, she regretted all the publicity she'd done to promote her fledgling business—the glider tutorial at the Holyoake County Fair, the aerial show during the Holyoake Fall Festival. Cutch was right. Everyone knew exactly what she did. And anyone who saw her flying over their drugmaking operation would logically conclude she not only saw them but was able to take pictures of what they were up to.

Ironically, Elise would have loved to be able to take pictures from her glider, but she'd never figured out a way to make it work. Too bad the gunmen hadn't known that.

Pinching back the terrifying thoughts that filled her mind, Elise focused on the job at hand. "Okay. We're coming up on where I think I lost my glider. I need you to get a lock on the spot with the GPS. Then I'll go back over the anhydrous tank, and you can capture the coordinates of that location, too." She quickly filled him in on how to use the GPS device.

With Cutch's help, they spotted the glider, and she got both coordinates in a short time.

Elise pointed them back toward the airfield. She didn't like what they'd learned. The idea that the gunmen might know her identity and want her dead was a chilling thought. Unfortunately, they seemed to know a lot more about her than she knew about them. That put her at a marked disadvantage.

The only good news was seeing an empty parking space where her uncle Leroy's truck had been sitting when she'd left. She didn't want to imagine how her uncle would react at finding a McCutcheon on his property. Both Leroy and her father made no apology for their blatant hatred toward the McCutcheon clan, and they seemed to despise Cutch worst of all.

"Looks like Leroy's gone for lunch," she said with relief as she brought the plane down in a smooth landing. "We can use the computer in the office to download those pictures. I want to see exactly what you saw."

"The pictures should show more than I was able to

see from the sky. I zoomed in on the tank as much as I could."

Elise was impressed he'd thought to do that. "Excellent. That will help us see details more clearly. Maybe we can find something else that will give us an indication of who we're dealing with."

She parked the plane, did a quick postflight check and hurried with Cutch to the office where the sign on the door informed them Leroy didn't expect to be back for another half hour. After making a mental note to be sure to be gone long before Leroy got back, Elise used her key to let them in.

As the pictures uploaded, she clicked through the shots of the Mitchum's corn maze, which appeared on the screen first.

"Wow," Cutch leaned over her shoulder as she sat in the only chair at the computer desk. "That's a complex maze they've got going on there."

Elise tried not to notice how closely he hovered behind her or the way her heart beat faster because he was there. "Yeah, they're pretty proud of it. It's their most complicated maze to date, and they've been doing this for fifteen years. That's why they wanted me to take pictures, although they're for next year's publicity—they don't want to give away the secrets of the maze to the general public. That would spoil all the fun."

"Makes sense," Cutch agreed in a whisper as Elise clicked through to the first shot of the pecan grove. The anhydrous tank was clearly visible, right down to the block letters on the side that identified its contents.

"Crazy," Elise murmured. "You'd think they'd at least cover the label."

"Nah," Cutch disagreed. "There's nothing illegal about having or using anhydrous ammonia. But the law requires the tanks to be correctly labeled as an inhalation hazard. If they were to transport that tank without it being labeled, it would only raise suspicions."

"And having anhydrous in a pecan grove wouldn't raise suspicions?"

"Not unless it's seen. I'm the only person who's ever out there, and that's rare enough."

"How did they even get it out there? It's thick trees all through there."

"There's an old road that runs through the middle of the section, but they're still a good stretch off that. The pecan trees are evenly spaced with plenty of room between them for a vehicle to pass. There's quite a bit of undergrowth in most places, but that doesn't mean they wouldn't be able to get in between it."

"Not without leaving a trail," Elise noted.

"Hopefully not," Cutch agreed. "I haven't been through that stretch since spring, so whatever marks we find are evidence as far as I'm concerned. We'll have to keep that in mind when we get out there."

"We?" Elise turned the swiveling office chair to face him. "You're planning to go out there with me?"

He glared down at her, already at a height advantage with his tall, lanky frame, the difference between them that much greater since he stood while she sat. "Yes, Elise. I'm going out there with you. I know the land. You don't. And you're going to need my help if you expect to get your glider out of the trees without damaging it any more than it already is."

Elise turned her chair back around—not because she needed to look at the computer screen again but because she needed to look away from Cutch. His good looks were distracting. "I'll call Sheriff Bromley. If he can't come out himself, I'm sure he'll send somebody. After all, we found the crime scene. The last thing we should do is tamper with it."

"Elise." The pleading way Cutch said her name twisted her heart.

She spun back around, angry that he could have so much power over her just by saying her name. "What?" she asked, scooting the chair back and standing. It wasn't fair that he should have such a height advantage, either. She leveled a glare at him. "Why don't you want the sheriff to investigate?"

"Because it's my land." His blue eyes looked stormy as he pinched his lips shut.

"So? I thought you were mad these guys were trespassing. I thought you wanted them caught. How is that going to happen if we don't get the authorities out there?"

Cutch ran his hands over his tired-looking face and back up through his hair, leaving the thick black waves shooting upward at odd angles. For a moment, Elise felt distracted by the attraction she felt toward him. Was it possible he was even better looking today than he'd been eight years before?

Stepping a little past her, Cutch leaned one leg against the computer desk and half sat on its sturdy steel surface. Now she had the height advantage.

"I'd like to believe," he began slowly, "the authorities will be able to catch whoever is behind this. But unless they can find evidence pointing to someone else, *I'm* going to be their main suspect."

"But you have no criminal record," she began, about to list off the many reasons why they'd never be able to pin the blame on him.

The look on his face gave her pause. He looked hurt. He looked *guilty.*

Elise gasped as she recalled a vicious rumor that had

circulated in the years after their romance had ended. She'd refused to listen to the gossip, and most of her friends knew better than to talk about Cutch anywhere around her, but she knew enough to remember the main theme. Cutch and drugs. Meth?

"Do you?" she asked softly.

He lifted his eyes to meet hers. Something in their blue depths begged for understanding. "I was a person of interest under investigation, but I was never arrested because they never found anything. There was nothing to find. I didn't do anything."

Elise took a step back and let out a slow breath. She knew better than to trust a McCutcheon. How many hundreds of times had she heard her father say, "There's nothin', no nothin' worse than a McCutcheon"? The rhythmic slant rhyme mimicked the old "a stitch in time saves nine" and "early to bed, early to rise makes a man healthy wealthy and wise," giving the phrase the same ageless voice of authority as those well-accepted aphorisms.

She *knew* better than to trust Cutch. She'd learned that lesson the hard way herself when he'd betrayed and humiliated her eight years before. But as she looked down at him perched there on the edge of the desk, took in the defeated slump of his broad shoulders under his worn T-shirt and watched his calloused hands sweep back through his hair again—sending it spiking up in an adorable mess—she felt her heart give a little groan. She wanted to believe him. She really did.

Cutch shook his head regretfully. "What am I doing? I'm not going to try to stop you from calling the sheriff. This is your *safety* we're talking about. I trust Sheriff Bromley to find the real offenders. Really, I do. Go ahead and call him."

Unsure what to do, Elise obediently pulled out her

phone, wishing she had more time to decide, to pray about what was the right thing to do. She flipped her phone open.

As her fingers poised above the number pad, Cutch's stomach gave a loud grumble. Elise looked at him with a wry smile. "Are you hungry?"

"Sorry about that," he quickly apologized, patting his toned midsection. "I had breakfast at five this morning, and now it's—"

"Well past noon," Elise said before him, already on her way to the fridge in the kitchenette corner of the office, wondering if she'd be crazy to offer him lunch. But *she* was hungry and needed to think, and she couldn't think on an empty stomach. Nor would she be so rude as to eat in front of a hungry man, even if he was a McCutcheon. She pulled out a foil-covered pan, glad to have an excuse not to have to make the call just yet. "Do you like lasagna?"

He grinned. "Of course I do. But you're not thinking of sharing your lunch with me, are you?"

Standing at the counter with her back to him, Elise pulled back the foil to reveal a huge pan of cold lasagna with only a couple of pieces missing. "Why not? The recipe always makes too much, and I get bored of the leftovers after about the fourth or fifth meal. This will help me use it up faster. Besides, we can't catch the bad guys on empty stomachs."

"I can't argue with that," he said amiably. Sincerity filled his voice. "Thank you, Elise. You really don't have to—"

She turned around, headed for the cupboard where they kept plates, not realizing he'd walked up behind her and was looking almost over her shoulder at the food. She was startled to see him so close to her. His hands steadied her arms.

"Oh!" she gasped, instantly aware of his closeness and the tension she'd felt between them all morning. She felt her heart rate revving up like an engine ready for takeoff. "I, uh—"

"Sorry about that," he apologized, but didn't let go of her.

"Plates," she said, not taking her eyes off his face. The once-so-familiar jawline angled toward her, his lips curved in an almost-amused expression, while his brow knit with a hint of concern.

"Plates," he repeated.

"In the cupboard," she whispered, her voice regrettably breathless as she gestured with a nod of her head toward where the plates were stashed.

Cutch dropped her arms. "What can I do to help?"

Elise turned away from him and pulled out the plates. "Um, drinks?" she suggested, taking a deep breath and telling herself whatever had just happened was nothing.

Too bad she didn't believe herself.

"There should be some tea in the fridge. Leroy always runs a fresh batch when he gets here in the mornings." Elise directed him to find glasses and tried to pretend nothing had happened between them. She nuked generous servings of the lasagna and focused on getting lunch on the table so they could be out of there before her uncle returned. Cutch helpfully placed forks and napkins at the tiny table beside the wall.

"I hope it's warm through," Elise apologized in advance as she carried the plates over.

"It smells delicious," Cutch assured her as she set the plates down and sat across from him, her knees all but brushing his. Reaching across the table, he surprised her by taking hold of her hand. "Mind if I bless it?"

The rough touch of his calloused fingers sent a shock

right up her arm. "S-sure," she nodded, unable to form a more coherent response, her mind mostly occupied with his warm touch. The man did crazy things to her heart. She pulled together her thoughts just enough to bow her head as Cutch sent up thanks to God not only for providing the meal but also for keeping Elise safe that morning. He ended with a plea that God would help them find her attackers and that God would keep them safe.

Cutch gave Elise's hand a final squeeze before releasing it as he said, "Amen."

Elise kept her head bowed and her eyes closed, though she pulled her hand back. How could she even consider that a man of prayer might be guilty of producing drugs or worse yet be associated with whoever had taken a shot at her that morning? Though they didn't go to the same church, Elise knew Cutch was actively involved in the church he'd been raised in. And though she knew some people resented the power Cutch held as county assessor, most of the people in Holyoake County respected him. It didn't fit that he'd be involved with the drugs, but she wasn't certain she could trust her own judgment.

Silently, she pleaded for God to guide her decisions, especially the decision of when to call the sheriff. Though the McAlisters had hated the McCutcheons for generations, she'd never forgive herself for sending one of them to jail—at least if he was innocent. How could she know?

Peeking her eyes open, she watched as Cutch took a bite of lasagna. He chewed for a second, smiled and looked up at her. After he swallowed, he pronounced, "Excellent. Did you make this yourself?"

She blushed at his appraisal and shrugged. "I do most of the cooking. After Mom left when I was six, Aunt Linda, Leroy's wife, used to bring us supper sometimes. At first I think she figured Dad would eventually remarry. When he never did, she decided her only hope of getting out of the job was if she trained me. Now I try to make it up to her by bringing meals out here, but Leroy likes to sneak off for fast food when he thinks he can get away with it." She dug into her lasagna and wondered why she'd shared so much. She didn't usually talk about her mother, but Cutch had a knack for making her babble.

He seemed to welcome her burst of sharing, too. "Do you ever hear from your mother?"

"We e-mail. She's happily married in Oklahoma and has three other kids. They're almost grown now, too. She'd like for me to come visit, but I just—" Elise caught herself before she shared any more. Why was Cutch so easy to talk to?

"That must be hard," he empathized.

"It's complicated," she agreed, hoping he'd leave it at that.

They ate in silence for a few more minutes until Cutch finished and wiped his mouth, setting his napkin atop his empty plate. "Thank you for the meal. It was delicious. We should be getting on our way. I can wash these dishes while you call the sheriff."

Elise froze, her last bite of lasagna poised on her fork midway to her mouth. She set it back down on her plate and looked into his eyes. Could she trust this man? Her father would say *no*. But her heart seemed to think otherwise. "I thought maybe we could wait to call the sheriff until we get out there and see what we're dealing with."

Cutch felt relief hit him like the first drops of rain after a long dry spell. Of course, he'd been nervous about what Sheriff Bromley might find on his land and what conclusions those findings would lead the lawman to reach. But more than that, Elise's words held a promise he'd been too hurt to even hope for. She trusted him, however slightly. She was willing to give him a chance, however small. Her concession soothed his parched soul.

But he couldn't let her jeopardize her safety on his account. He shook his head. "I can't ask you to put off calling him. It was selfish of me to voice my fears to you. Go ahead and make the call. Your safety could be at stake."

Elise finished her last bite of lasagna and offered him a tiny smile. "The sheriff already told me he was busy today. By calling him once we've been out there to see what we're dealing with, we might actually be able to save him time on his investigation. I'm not risking my safety—not at this point. Once we find something for him to look at, then I'll give him a call."

"But we already have the coordinates for the location of the ammonia tank."

"And I already gave you my answer." She rose and carried their dishes to the sink.

Guilt hit him like a punch to the stomach. Why had he even said anything? Unless Elise had changed dramatically in the eight years since he'd last been involved with her, he knew once she'd made up her mind that she wouldn't budge. And everything from her body language to the glint in her eyes told him she'd made up her mind.

"If anything happens to you—" he began.

"I'm trusting you to protect me," she said, her back to him as she ran water to wash their plates. "Now if you don't mind, there's a ladder just inside the hangar we were in earlier. If you load that into your truck, we can use it to help us reach my glider."

Cutch's shoulders dropped. "Sure thing," he answered, knowing he'd been dismissed. Reluctantly, he turned and left her behind, wondering if he shouldn't just call the sheriff on his own. But she'd be *furious* with him if she felt he'd gone behind her back. Whatever tiny bit of trust she'd placed in him would be lost.

I'm trusting you to protect me. Her words filled his heart with a mixture of joy and dread. He felt honored she'd grant him that responsibility, but at the same time, he wondered if he was really up to the challenge. He couldn't bear the idea of letting Elise down again.

His mind swirling with all the risks that still lay ahead of them, Cutch headed straight for the hangar without going around the side of the office to see if Leroy's truck was back, though the time he'd stated for his return had passed a few minutes before. Instead, Cutch hurried inside to fetch the ladder. After the bright Iowa sunshine outside, his eyes took a moment to adjust to the relative darkness of the metal building's spacious interior.

As his eyes adjusted, he scanned the walls for the ladder Elise had talked about. He saw an aluminum ladder along one wall and headed over, picking it up and hefting it above his shoulder.

Just as Cutch began to turn around, Leroy's voice boomed through the cavernous room, "Well, I'll be! Is that a rat or a McCutcheon? I wouldn't waste a bullet trying to shoot a rat, but I would if that's a McCutcheon there." The sound of clicking metal echoed through the hangar. "Drop the ladder, boy."

FOUR

Something nagged Elise as she finished washing up the dishes—something uncomfortable. She tried to shake the feeling—to tell herself she was just jittery after being shot out of the sky and forced to spend her morning with Cutch. Just thinking about Cutch made her feel off-kilter. But the knot in her stomach couldn't be so easily explained away.

Feeling distracted by everything on her mind, she finished rinsing their plates, set the clean dishes on angle in the drying rack and carried the soapy sponge over to the table. When the table's clean surface gleamed up at her, she spun around to return to the sink, and something caught her eye outside the window.

Something red. Her heart jolted, but she told herself it was nothing. Only Leroy's truck. She'd seen it sitting in that spot a thousand times before. He'd probably step into the office any second. She had the sponge back at the sink and was rinsing it out when the tangible sense of fear hit her. Leroy hadn't come into the office—which meant he was still outside, or worse yet, in the hangar. With Cutch.

Elise dropped the sponge and ran. She tore around the corner of the hangar and sprinted inside. "Leroy, no!" she shouted, mortified to see her uncle pointing a shotgun at Cutch.

"Caught this varmint trying to steal our ladder," the big man snarled, not tearing his eyes from his prey.

Cutch glared at them both but remained silent.

Silence was probably a good strategy on his part, Elise decided. She quickly moved to stand between Leroy and Cutch. "It's okay, Uncle Leroy. I asked him to get the ladder."

"You asked a McCutcheon to steal our ladder?" Leroy didn't even lower his gun. "Now that don't make any sense at all. This boy's been addling your brain again, child."

Elise did not appreciate having her uncle talk down to her, even if he'd been right about Cutch before. She also wished he'd put the gun down. Since she'd gone to stand between them, he now had the barrel aimed at her as well as Cutch. "He's helping me," she explained slowly. "My glider went down on his land, and he offered to help me retrieve it."

Leroy lowered the gun slightly, concern softening the anger in his voice. "Your glider went down?"

"Yes. And I'm kind of in a hurry to get it back. It may take us a while, and you know I don't like to leave it out overnight—dew isn't good for the body or the engine." Buckshot was even worse, but she hoped her uncle would let her skip over the longer, more detailed version of the story.

His eyes narrowed, Leroy held his ground. "I don't like the sound of that. Your glider went down over McCutcheon land—"

"Leroy!" Elise couldn't let her uncle continue questioning her. If he found out she'd been shot down, he'd never let her leave with Cutch. "It's okay. I know what I'm doing.

But we have to get going, okay?" She met his eyes. "Can you just trust me on this?"

Grumbling, Leroy looked past her to Cutch. "You take and load that ladder, but I expect to get it back by sundown or you'll wish I'd just shot you!"

Elise had to stop herself from rolling her eyes. Her uncle could be such a throwback sometimes. "Thank you, Uncle Leroy," she said calmly as she began to follow Cutch out the door.

Leroy caught her arm. "You be careful out there, honey."

Elise saw the concern in her uncle's brown eyes and realized he referred to more than just her safety. Leroy was familiar with enough of her history with Cutch to know her heart was in just as much danger as the rest of her. Probably more.

"We'll be fine," she assured him with a smile she only wished she felt. Grabbing her portable GPS unit and the storage bag for her glider, she hurried toward Cutch's truck. Would she be fine? She could only pray she would.

Cutch had to ignore his curiosity about the anhydrous tank he'd seen. Much as he wanted to check out the site they'd spotted from the air, he knew Elise was in a hurry to get her glider out of the trees, and he'd already risked her safety by agreeing to postpone the phone call to the sheriff. He could investigate the drug lab later once she was safely home and unlikely to return.

"Thanks for telling your uncle not to shoot me," he said after they'd driven in silence for over a mile.

"I didn't have much choice, did I? If he'd killed you, there's no way I could have gotten my glider back today."

Her words came out in a perfectly serious voice, but

when Cutch looked over, he thought he caught a hint of
a smile. He fought back a grin. "Worse yet, if he'd have
wounded me, you might have had to do CPR." Expecting her to slug him for such a bold comment, he braced
himself for the impact of her little fist.

"Nah. I'd have made Leroy do the mouth-to-mouth.
He's the one with the EMT training." She shot him a look
and laughed at the horrified expression he gave her in
return.

Cutch tipped his head back and chuckled, too. It felt so
good to laugh with Elise, especially after the stress-filled
day they'd had so far. "Then I'm glad he didn't shoot me
after all." He glanced her way. She had her eyes trained
out the window, and her slender fingers played nervously
with the shoulder strap of her seatbelt. Her laughter had
already faded.

Tension settled back over them. He felt it like a thick
choking cloud, the same elephant in the room that had
always come between them. And though his logical side
knew it would always be there—knew they'd never overcome the chasm between them—he couldn't help praying
God would show him the way past all that.

"So, pecans, hmm?" Elise's question drew him back
from his thoughts.

Cutch's instinct was to clam up. Not even his folks
knew what his plans were, and he wasn't expecting to
tell anyone, either, not until he knew if his plans would
succeed. Eight years ago, he'd let his guard down with
Elise and shared his dream with her. She was the only
one besides his younger sister, Ginny, who knew what
he'd wanted. Would it be okay to let her know how far
he'd come? Sharing went against his secretive nature.

"Yeah," he replied in a noncommittal voice and kept
his eyes focused on the road in front of them.

"Those trees looked pretty old. One of them had a dead branch, as I recall."

She was baiting him. Cutch warred with what to tell her. *Nobody* in Holyoake County knew what his plans were—and for good reason. If people thought he was foolish enough to believe in his grandfather's ruined dream of converting the otherwise infertile hills into a productive pecan farm, they'd never believe he could do an adequate job as county assessor. He was up for reelection again this fall. He could lose his job.

"About sixty years old," he told her quietly, wondering how he could possibly change the subject without raising her suspicions. Who was he kidding? This was Elise. She already knew enough to be suspicious.

"Over six hundred acres of pecan trees." She said it like a statement, not a question, her words quiet, unobtrusive.

She knew.

To spare her from digging any deeper, he came right out and admitted, "Grandpa's." He took the next corner quietly, and they began to close in on the property.

"You bought it all?"

"Yup."

"Congratulations," her voice stayed soft, calm. "I hope it works out for you. If anyone can make it work, you can."

Like taking his work boots off after a long day, like loosening his belt after a huge Thanksgiving feast, something inside his soul gave a long-suppressed sigh at her words. She believed in him? She'd said so eight years ago, but he'd figured—

"You have any success with it yet?" she interrupted his thoughts.

"Not really. The trees are strong, just not productive."

Though he hoped Elise would know better, he felt he had to say, "Don't mention the pecan trees to anyone, okay?" He glanced over at her.

"I never have." She returned his look. "Although I don't see why you have to be so secretive about it."

Cutch looked back at the road. "Everybody knows loess soil isn't good for anything," he explained. "If people thought I was deluded enough to think it was good for growing pecans, they'd not only figure I was crazy but they might decide I don't know enough about land value to be the county assessor after all."

"Oh." Elise filled that lone syllable with understanding. "You don't think—"

"I didn't win the last election by a very large margin. And county assessors tend to make enemies faster than they make friends."

"Oh." The syllable came out an octave lower this time, as though weighed down by the gravity of his words. "I won't say a thing about the pecan trees, Cutch. Or your plans."

"Thanks." For all the bad blood between their families, Cutch knew Elise would be true to her word. When he looked her way again, she had her eyes on the trees before them.

Cutch turned onto the road where he'd picked up Elise, which ran along the north end of the property. He headed in from the west, on the far end from where he'd spotted the anhydrous tank. Somewhere in the trees south of them they'd find Elise's glider. Unless the gunmen found them first.

Elise had her portable GPS out and watched the screen as it counted down their longitudinal progress.

"Right about here," she said.

Cutch slowed the truck to a stop off to the side of the

road a bit. He hopped out and grabbed the ladder from where he'd stored it in back. Elise pulled out the neatly folded nylon bag that she'd explained would carry the folded glider.

"Ready?" he asked.

She had her eyes on the GPS screen but looked up at him and smiled. "Ready."

They found a stretch where the brambles and bushes weren't too thick, and Cutch used the ladder to hold down the barbed wire fence as they climbed over. He had a tricky time keeping the ladder from getting caught up in low-hanging branches, but Elise helped by going ahead with the GPS and holding branches back for him to carry the ladder through. They tromped in relative silence until she said, "Okay, we should be closing in on it soon. Up this way." She pointed down the valley.

Cutch looked up through the treetops and soon caught a glimpse of yellow and red fabric fluttering in the wind. They hurried over, and a moment later, he blinked up into the treetop at her mangled glider.

"Is it salvageable?" he asked skeptically.

Elise sounded a little worried, too. "I sure hope so. The Labor Day Powered Glider Festival is Monday down in the Kansas City area. Before this happened I was planning to drive down tomorrow. I guess I still hoped I might be able to get her patched back together in time to go on Monday."

"That's the day after tomorrow," Cutch mused, then looked over and saw the disappointment on Elise's face. "I'm sure it won't look so bad once we get it out of the tree." He leaned the ladder against a bough and circled around, trying to assess what the best approach might be.

When he turned back around, Elise was on the ladder.

"Hold on, now," he ran over and steadied the ladder. "I didn't put that there to climb on. You could tip and fall and hurt yourself."

"It's fine. I'm going to pull myself up onto the next branch." Elise stepped off the ladder onto a solid-looking limb and began climbing up the tree branches from there.

"Careful," Cutch warned from the ground.

"It might surprise you to know I actually jumped out of this tree earlier today, from over there," she gestured to where her cut harness straps dangled a few branches away. "I was fine then, and I'll be fine now." As she spoke, she made her way out onto the long limb where the lower parts of her glider were ensnared.

Cutch watched, feeling futile, while Elise teased the torn fabric free, snapping off twigs and leaves and dropping them to the ground. "Can I come up there and help you?"

"Don't bother. I doubt this branch could hold both of us, and besides, I'm making pretty good progress." She'd made it to where the aluminum frame scissored through the smaller branches. After some futile tugging, she sighed. "I don't suppose you have any pruning shears or a small saw or something? I just need to get these branches out of here."

"Actually, I have saws, clippers, shears, you name it—in my truck. Want me to run back and fetch some?"

Elise made a face at the branches and sighed again. "Yes. If you don't mind."

"I'll be right back. Just don't hurt yourself while I'm gone."

"I'll try not to."

As Cutch turned to hurry off, he glanced up at Elise and saw her smiling down at him. As soon as she saw him looking back, her smile disappeared. He hurried off to his truck with a grin on his face. Elise McAlister had been smiling at him. It was enough to make a grown man giddy.

The underbrush was thick, and in his haste, Cutch didn't bother trying to move quietly. He crashed through the woods, rounding the hillside and coming up on where he'd left his truck. Branches snapped and leaves rattled as he hurried toward it. He didn't see the other vehicle until it began to pull away.

Cutch froze. A red pickup sped away from where it had stopped beside his truck. He tried to get a glimpse inside, but the driver must have heard him coming, because he sped off in a cloud of dust.

He tried to get a peek at the license plate, but between the dust cloud and the branches blocking his view, he couldn't even see enough of the truck to determine a make or model. By the time he broke free of the snarled bushes, the truck had disappeared over the next hill.

Clambering over the fence, Cutch hurried out onto the road. Tire tracks crisscrossed through the sparse gravel. He couldn't begin to sort out which ones may have belonged to the vehicle. After he caught his breath, he wondered if the pickup he'd seen had actually been stopped by his, or if in his paranoia he'd only imagined it. It would be easy enough to tell himself the encounter had meant nothing—that the red truck was simply another vehicle passing through the remote area on business of its own.

But that was just it. They were in a remote area. The only people who'd likely be passing by were the owners of the neighboring properties, and most of them tended to use the next road south, which was better maintained and less hilly. Cutch rarely used this road unless he was working on the north end of his land as he had been early that

morning before he'd picked up Elise. Besides, he didn't
know of any neighbors who drove a red pickup truck.

It didn't take Cutch long to grab a handful of the useful
sawing and pruning tools he still had stowed in his truck
from his work that morning. He hurried back, relieved to
find Elise still clinging to the branch by her glider. She'd
even managed to free more of the other wing while he'd
been gone.

"You know anybody who drives a red truck?" he asked
as he drew closer.

She laughed at him. "A whole lot of people drive
red trucks. Both Rodney and Leroy have red trucks. Ed
McClinton down the road from us, too, but his is kind of
a burgundy-red. What shade are you looking for?"

"More of a cherry-red."

"Bernie Gills, the sheriff's deputy, drives a cherry-
red truck. And doesn't your grandpa Scarth have a red
truck?"

"That's right." Though he was in his late eighties,
Cutch's mother's father still drove regularly and preferred
to stick to the back roads where there was less traffic. He'd
even have an innocent excuse for stopping if he thought
he'd recognized Cutch's pickup. But it wouldn't have made
sense for him to have driven off in a hurry if he'd heard
him coming or for him to have been out on this end of the
county.

"Why do you ask?"

"I saw a red truck stopped near mine when I came out
of the woods. It drove off in a hurry." He saw the worry
on her face and realized he might be scaring her for no
reason. Elise had enough on her mind as it was. Cutch
injected a lighthearted tone into his voice. "It's probably
nothing."

Elise wasn't so easily dissuaded. "How many people use that road?"

"It's a public road," Cutch said dismissively, not wanting to worry her. He held up the assortment of saws and clippers. "Which of these do you want to use?"

Elise frowned at him and then scowled back at the tree branches. "Toss me that little folding handsaw. That should do it."

After leaning the other tools against the base of the tree and carefully collapsing and securing the blade inside the saw's handle so Elise wouldn't cut herself with it, Cutch tossed it gently into the air in her direction.

Elise's fingertips brushed it as it flew near, but then it dropped to the ground again. "Almost. Good toss. Try it again. I'll see if I can't lean out farther."

"Be careful," he warned her as the saw left his hand.

The next toss was even better, delivering the saw gently to the airspace right in front of her. She clamped her hand around the end, fumbled for a hold and somehow, in her efforts to grab it, let go of the tree branch with her other hand. She tottered on edge for a second as the saw began its downward descent.

"Elise!" Cutch shouted as she began to fall. Without thinking he stepped forward, arms stretched wide, and caught her as she came down.

"Oof!"

He fell backward, pinned to the ground by a red-faced Elise.

"What are you doing?" she screeched at him. "Are you okay? I didn't hurt you, did I?"

Momentarily winded, Cutch took a second to drag in a deep breath and took the liberty of brushing a clump of leaves from Elise's hair with his fingertips. "I'm okay. Are you okay?" Her hair felt silky under his fingers, which

weren't used to touching anything so soft. He tucked the
ends back behind her ear as he had so often seen her do.

Elise froze, sprawled awkwardly across Cutch's shoulders with her knees buried in the leaves beside him and
more leaves half covering her. She didn't care about the
leaves or the dirt or even the fact that she'd landed with
such an awful thump.

Cutch had his fingers in her hair. His hand all but
cupped her cheek as he tucked her hair behind her ear.
His well-muscled chest rose and fell as he sucked in air
after the hard landing. The startled birds had begun to
sing again by the time Elise pulled her rattled brain back
to earth.

"Sorry about that. I almost had it," she apologized,
taking inventory of her hands and deciding they weren't
too dirty to press against his shoulders as she tried to push
herself up.

All she had to do was put her hands on his shoulders
and push herself up. She could do this.

"Are you sure you're okay?" Concern filled Cutch's
vivid blue eyes.

Okay? She was in the arms of the man she loved. Of
course she was—

"No." She shook her head. She didn't love him! She
must have hit her head harder than she'd thought.

Cutch rolled on to his side and cradled her on his arm.
He brushed the side of her face with his fingers. "Are you
experiencing dizziness? Double vision?" He pulled his
hands away and held up three fingers. "How many fingers
am I holding up?"

Elise pulled her eyes away from his face long enough
to look at his hand. "Three."

A relieved-looking smile passed over his face. "Good. Are you feeling better? Ready to try standing?"

Mortified that she'd let their encounter continue, Elise nodded and scooted onto her feet while Cutch took both of her hands and pulled her to a standing position. She forced herself to stand steadily, though the strong tug of his arms almost tipped her back against him again. She couldn't let that happen.

"I'm okay," she assured him and turned her back to him, heading for the ladder.

"Whoa, no you don't," Cutch said, tugging on the hand he still held.

"I have to get my glider down," Elise reminded him, frustrated that she was still on the ground, wasting time with him, when she needed to be in the tree freeing her glider. The fact that he had hold of her hand didn't help matters any, either.

"I'll do it."

"That's really not necessary—"

"Elise," he interrupted, "you fell out of the tree. Not two minutes ago you were very shaken up and even a little disoriented. If I let you go up there again, you could fall and hurt yourself even worse this time."

As much as Elise wanted to protest, to tell him she really hadn't been all that shaken up, such a confession would require explaining the real reason she'd felt so disoriented—because of her lingering attraction to him. And there was no way she'd admit that. "Fine." She fumed. "Let me hold the ladder for you."

Cutch shoved the collapsible handsaw into his back pocket and headed up. "I'll have this down in no time," he said as he began his ascent.

Unfortunately, "no time" ended up being almost two hours by the time Cutch freed the entire glider and handed it down in two pieces. Elise was further disheartened when she inspected the damage and discovered she wouldn't be able to attend the Labor Day Powered Glider Festival after all—not as a participant, anyway.

"I'm sorry," Cutch commiserated when Elise voiced her disappointment. "Do they have a festival every year?"

"Yes," Elise admitted as they hoofed the ladder and what remained of her glider out of the woods. The sun had dipped below the level of the steep hills and so, though a few hours of daylight remained, the valley, at least, was cast in shadows. "It's just that I have friends there I was hoping to see. And it's always such fun." She didn't want to share all of her feelings with Cutch, but she'd always been sheltered by her overprotective father, and going to the festival was one of the few opportunities she had, besides flying itself, to get away and be herself.

"I'm sorry," Cutch repeated. "Is there any way I could make it up to you?"

Elise paused to catch her breath from carrying the cumbersome equipment over the uneven terrain. She looked up at him and felt a familiar tug on her heart. "Just take me home," she said and sighed.

For a second, disappointment crossed Cutch's face, but he quickly set his jaw in a stony expression and turned in the direction they were headed. "Sure thing."

The guilty squeeze in her chest told Elise she shouldn't be so cold toward him, but at the same time, after the trouble she'd had pulling herself away from him when she fell on him out of the tree, she felt as though she had to push him away. For both their sakes.

They trudged silently toward the truck, and Cutch held the barbed wire fence down again for her to cross over. He tossed the ladder in the back of his truck and helped her stow her glider, unlocking and opening her door before circling around to the driver's side.

Sore and thirsty, Elise sighed as she climbed into the truck. "I can't wait to get home."

Cutch's voice carried from the other side of the truck. "I'm afraid you're going to have to wait."

She looked out the driver's side window to find him glaring down at something near the ground. "Why?" she asked with dread in her voice.

"I have two flat tires."

"You're kidding. Did we run over a bunch of nails or something?"

"Nope." Cutch crouched down and inspected the front tire. "They've been slashed."

FIVE

"No," Elise protested, scooting over to the driver's side door and hopping out. "On purpose?"

Cutch scowled at the four-inch slice in the thick rubber. "Had to have been. These are newer tires, too. I bet it was that red truck I saw."

Elise swallowed back the fear she felt rising in her throat. "They might have done all four tires if they hadn't heard you coming."

"I guess I should be glad they got scared off instead of attacking me." Cutch let out a long breath and shook his head. "I've only got one spare."

Elise anxiously swept her hair back behind her ears. Normally she'd offer to call someone to bring them another tire, but she didn't want anyone to know she was out with Cutch. "I think it's time to call the sheriff."

With his head under her glider as he hauled the spare tire out of the back of the truck, Cutch's grumble was muffled but no less disgusted. "Have him call Gary's Garage, too, or at least have him give you the number and I'll call him. Maybe he can bring us another tire." He tossed the spare down, and it bounced a couple of times before settling on its side.

It didn't take long for them to complete the calls, and

soon both the sheriff and Gary were on their way. Elise looked up at Cutch worriedly as he got off the phone with the man from the garage. "How much do you want to tell the sheriff?" she asked quietly.

Both of them turned to look at the thick trees, which were cast in lengthening shadows, whose dark depths could hide secrets. Or gunmen. Elise shivered, though the late summer evening was still warm.

"I suppose we'll have to tell him about the anhydrous tank." Cutch pinched his lips into a thin line. "I'd like to get a chance to look at that site first, but I won't be going anywhere for a while." He looked pointedly at the slashed tires.

"And whoever did this knows it, too." Elise wished she didn't feel like such a sitting duck. "Don't they?"

Cutch must have felt the same way, because he looked warily around them and took a step closer to her, lowering his voice. "If I don't tell the sheriff about the site and he finds out later, it will look like I was withholding information. That will only make me look guiltier."

Elise began to reach for his arm, but at the last second she corralled her compassionate instincts and shoved her hands into her pockets. She wished she could think of something to say that would make him feel better, but the only thing she could think of was to tell him she still believed in him. And even if that was true, which she wasn't convinced of, she didn't want to say anything to align herself with him any more than she already had. McCutcheons were dangerous. Why was that so difficult for her to remember?

Instead she asked, "Want me to help you change the tire?"

"Not yet. I don't know if it will make any difference, but since the sheriff is going to be here any minute, we might as well let him look at the tires the way we found them. Maybe we'll get lucky and he'll recognize the handiwork."

Elise offered a strained smile in exchange for his optimistic outlook. Before long, they saw the sheriff's vehicle topping a nearby hill. They stood at attention, waiting as Sheriff Bromley pulled up, his dark eyes on the slashed tires from the moment he stepped out of his cruiser.

Elise stood back while Gideon Bromley interviewed Cutch. Though the sheriff wasn't even a decade older than she was, he was the youngest son of a large Holyoake family, and he had older siblings who were her dad's age. So he still managed to resonate capability and reassurance, even if he wasn't the most experienced member of the department. Gideon Bromley was someone she'd always respected and trusted, and she felt some of the tension that had built up over the day start to recede as Cutch explained to the sheriff all that had happened that day, including their discovery of the anhydrous tank.

"I'd like to see those pictures," the sheriff said, tucking his pen back into his chest pocket.

"They're on the computer at the airfield office," Elise explained as a Gary's Garage truck pulled to a stop behind the sheriff's cruiser.

"Then that's where we'll head next," Gideon Bromley told her, "as soon as we get these tires changed."

While Cutch and Gary started in on the tires, the sheriff got on his radio. Elise could hear him updating whoever was on the other end—probably the dispatcher—about where he was going to be. Cutch started quizzing Gary on who he knew of who drove a cherry-red truck, having explained to the older mechanic about how his tires had been slashed.

"Who drives a red truck in this county?" Gary repeated

the question. "Dozens of people, maybe even hundreds. I could go through my records and give you a list if you think it will help."

The sheriff finished his conversation on the radio and stepped over. "Red trucks," he inserted himself back into the conversation. "We could do a thorough computer search with the county vehicle registrations. But boys, you've got to remember who owns the truck and who drives it might be two different people. Mayor Wilkins owns a red truck, but it's his son you always see driving it. My brother Bruce has a red truck, too, but he's got a fleet of other vehicles he's just as likely to drive, and any of his employees might drive the red truck. As far as leads go, the connection with a red truck is about as helpful as saying the perpetrator had a knife big enough to slash your tires with. Most everybody has access to a knife like that. Just like anybody could get their hands on a red truck."

While the sheriff spoke, Cutch and Gary finished changing the tires, and Gary loaded the slashed tires into his truck before promising to send Cutch a bill. Cutch thanked the man for his help before Gary drove off.

When the three of them were alone again, the sheriff shook his head. "If it weren't already dark out, I'd head into those woods with you two to see what you saw. But it's in such a remote area it would be hard to bring adequate lighting out there, and at this point we'd probably just mess up the crime scene."

"Do you want to take a look at it tomorrow?" Cutch asked.

"Tomorrow's Sunday," the sheriff replied in a thoughtful voice. "And it's Labor Day weekend. My staff is stretched tight, and I've got somewhere important I need to be, but I guess I could be a little late. You give me a call after church, and we'll see what we can find. For now, our best clue is those pictures you took. You two want to lead the way to the airstrip?"

Cutch and Elise hopped into the truck, and the sheriff followed in his cruiser. As Elise had expected, the lights were all off when they pulled in front of the airfield office. While Cutch unloaded Leroy's ladder, Elise hurried to the door and let them in with her key, turning on the lights and heading straight for the computer, which was still turned on. She roused the sleeping monitor to find her photo file still dominating the screen.

"Here are the pictures we downloaded today," she explained, clicking through the aerial shots of the corn maze. As she came to the last of the corn maze pictures, however, she was surprised to find herself clicking back through the first of the corn maze pictures.

Cutch gave her a worried look. She clicked through the pictures again. "That's strange," she muttered when the shots they'd taken over the pecan grove failed to appear.

"What's strange?" the sheriff asked.

"The pictures of the anhydrous tank are gone."

Cutch felt the worry pouring off Elise as she tried to locate the missing files. "How odd," she whispered under her breath. "Maybe they didn't download correctly." She grabbed the camera and plugged it back in to the universal port. "Let me try downloading them again."

As they waited on the computer, Cutch felt a sick feeling of dread fill him. When a message popped up on the screen announcing that the camera's files were empty, Cutch wasn't really that surprised.

Elise spun to face him, "You didn't erase the camera's memory card once we'd downloaded the pictures, did you?"

"No." Cutch took a step back, disappointed that she'd

so quickly place the blame on him, though he knew he shouldn't ultimately be surprised. "I wouldn't do that without asking you first."

Sheriff Bromley quickly intervened. "Okay, you two. Just step back from the computer. If those pictures got erased, whoever did it probably left fingerprints, so don't touch anything else. Elise, who has access to this office?"

"Uncle Leroy and Rodney Miller. Aunt Linda comes in once in a while, and anybody who has business setting up a field spray or paying their bill. This is a public business, after all, though a lot of our regulars set things up over the phone. But when the doors are unlocked, anybody can come in here."

"But the doors were locked when we arrived, correct?" Gideon Bromley pressed.

"Yes."

"Was anyone else in here that you know of—in particular, when the pictures were being downloaded?"

"Well, of course *I* was." Elise hesitated. "And Cutch."

Cutch heard the fear underpinning her words and realized how much the overwhelming events of the day must be piling up on her. He wanted to help. "I know. Elise, call your uncle and find out who came in today," he suggested.

"Good idea." The sheriff nodded. "I'm going to see what I can do about lifting fingerprints from the computer. I'll take a full set of prints on you two, too, so we can rule those out."

While Elise got on the phone and the sheriff ran back out to his cruiser to get the tools he needed, Cutch stepped back out of the way, his mind spinning. He prayed God would help them sort out what was going on. Everything seemed to be going from bad to worse, but nothing pointed toward any suspects—other than him.

Leaning one shoulder against the tall file cabinet set back in the corner near the window, Cutch felt the cool breeze that fluttered against the faded curtains. Something in the back of his mind stirred. It was odd, he thought after a while, that Leroy would have locked up the building but left the window open. Wondering if perhaps he ought to close it, Cutch looked down.

Broken glass littered the floor.

"Okay, then. Thanks, Uncle Leroy." Elise hung up the phone and met his eyes.

"What did you find out?" he asked her.

"Nobody."

Cutch cringed but kept his eyes locked on hers. "Come over here and take a look at this, but be careful where you step."

"What is it?"

Pointing to the broken glass, Cutch asked, "Was this window broken earlier?"

Elise's eyes widened, and she shook her head. "No. I think we would have noticed if it had been."

Cutch called to the sheriff, "We've got a broken window here. You might want to take more fingerprints."

They spent another hour at the office with the sheriff before Cutch finally dropped off Elise close enough to her house that she could carry her wounded glider home but still far enough away that her father wouldn't see who she'd been with. Cutch wasn't sure how the woman figured on keeping the day's events a secret—especially not after her phone calls to her uncle Leroy—but he wasn't about to protest when she placed her request. She'd had a long enough day. They both had.

Cutch arrived home hungry and tired a full twelve hours after his father's scheduled checkup—the one he'd said he'd be there for. He found his mother scrubbing away at her already-impeccably clean kitchen. That was how she dealt with his father's cancer. She cleaned things, as though by scrubbing away every last fallen crumb and speck of dust behind the stove and under the refrigerator, she could somehow erase the invasive cancer.

His heart went out to her.

"How is he?" Cutch asked.

Looking up from where she was bent over scrubbing the faces of the cupboards, Anita McCutcheon gave him a weary smile. "Resting. He had a good day today. He's tired."

"And you?"

"Not tired enough to sleep." She washed her hands at the sink. "Did you have supper?"

Cutch's stomach growled. "There wasn't time."

"I made pork chops, green beans and red potatoes."

"I can heat it up." Cutch headed her off as she stepped toward the fridge. "So, what did the nurse have to say?" he asked as he fixed a plate for himself and popped it into the microwave.

Anita McCutcheon shrugged. "He's not going to get better. But then we knew that. Right now it's just a matter of time."

"Did she say how long?" Though he didn't want to press the issue, Cutch needed to know what to expect. He'd given up his apartment in town three years before to move back out to the family farm to help his folks when his father had been diagnosed with cancer for the second time. His father had fought it back then, but before Cutch had the chance to move back into town, the cancer had returned with a vengeance. And Henry McCutcheon III had chosen not to fight back with another round of chemo. His condition had been steadily declining.

"Might be a few weeks, maybe even months. It's hard to say with cancer. The nurse says she's not surprised by anything anymore. And your dad's a fighter."

"That he is," Cutch concurred, digging into his dinner. So there wasn't much time. At one point, Cutch had hoped to clear his grandfather's name before his father died, so his father would know his own father hadn't been a total failure. But the way things were going, he didn't see how that could possibly happen. The odds were stacked against them both.

Eager to change the subject, Cutch raised an issue that had been bothering him ever since he'd seen the red truck driving away earlier. "Have you talked to Grandpa Scarth today?" He knew his mother tended to maintain daily contact with her aging father, and he hoped she'd be able to give him a clear alibi for the afternoon.

Instead, his mother scowled and shook her head. "I don't know what he's been up to. Lately he's never home, and when he answers his cell phone—which isn't often— he always sounds preoccupied and in a hurry to get back to what he was doing."

Cutch didn't like the sound of that. "Does he still drive that red truck everywhere?"

"Yes." Anita let out a frustrated breath. "And too fast, too. You'd think he was seventeen instead of eighty-seven."

Swallowing another bite of pork chop, Cutch asked, "So you don't know what he's been up to?"

"I've asked. He won't tell me." She sighed. "He's a grown man. I guess he's entitled to keep his secrets."

"I guess," Cutch agreed. His grandfather could do whatever he wanted—as long as he wasn't up to something illegal.

Elise stashed her glider in the barn before letting herself in the back door of the old farmhouse where she'd been raised. There were plusses and minuses to continuing to live in her dad's house. On the plus side, it allowed her to save money for her aerial photography business and the new plane she hoped to buy, while at the same time, helping her father with cooking and household chores. But on the definite minus side, it meant she was still under his oppressively overprotective thumb.

The kitchen was dark and quiet, and Elise poked her head into the refrigerator, wishing she'd thought to bring the pan of lasagna back home with her. She found some cold, charred burgers in a plastic bag on the top shelf. Her dad had been grilling again. As she opened the bag, memories came back, like they always did, at the smell of the grilled meat.

She hadn't known her mother would be leaving. Sure, her mom had taken "trips" before, when she'd disappear for days at a time, leaving Elise alone with her father and his limited cooking skills. Grilling was one of the few ways Bill McAlister could reliably prepare a decent meal. In retrospect, she'd often wondered why the fact that her dad had been grilling hadn't tipped her off to the possibility that she wouldn't see her mother again for four years.

Because she trusted people too much, that was why.

Elise stuck a slice of cheese atop a burger, placed it on a plate and let it warm in the microwave until the cheese was just melted. The smell hit her again when she opened the microwave door, the burnt odor of abandonment.

Her mother had rejected her. Though Elise had seen the strength of the mother-daughter bond between other mothers and their girls, for whatever reason, her mother hadn't loved her enough to stay. Or even to take her with her when she went.

Twenty-three years later, the disappointment was still strong enough to make the burger in her mouth taste like charcoal briquettes.

That, and her father really wasn't a very good cook.

Ravenous enough to eat even the charred burger, Elise choked down the last couple bites and tiptoed down the hall toward the stairs. As she passed by the living room, she saw the dim glow of a lamp and paused.

"Elise?" Her father looked up from his Bible and peeled back the wire-framed reading glasses that perched on the end of his nose.

"Hey, Dad. I hope you weren't waiting up for me." Elise didn't stay out late often, and she was pretty sure she'd outgrown a curfew by the time she'd left her teenage years.

"Leroy called."

"Did he wake you?"

Bill McAlister ignored the question. "He told me who you were with. Elise, there's nothin', no nothin'—"

"Worse than a McCutcheon," Elise finished the phrase in rhythm with her father. "I know, Dad. But sometimes in life you have to work with people you don't like."

"You don't like Young Cutch?"

"Of course not," Elise tried to convince herself her words weren't a lie. She *didn't* like Cutch. She might still feel some residual attraction toward him but not on purpose, and anyway, that was a lot different than liking him. Wasn't it? "I need to get to bed. I'm exhausted."

"Fine." Her father slid his reading glasses back into place but looked over their top rim with a firm warning in his eyes. "Just be careful, honey. You can't ever trust a McCutcheon."

"I know."

Elise hurried to her room, taking a moment before she shut down her computer to send an e-mail to her friends who'd be at the Labor Day Powered Glider Festival, letting them know she wouldn't be able to make it after all. Then she dragged her exhausted body through her nighttime routine. Through it all, her mind spun with her father's warning and the sheriff's assessment of the break-in at the airport office.

Sheriff Bromley had confiscated the airfield office computer in an attempt to try to retrieve the files, but Elise was fairly certain the pictures Cutch had taken of the anhydrous tank were irretrievably gone. The sheriff himself had made plans to meet them both in the pecan grove to investigate the tank itself right after church the next day. He'd said he didn't have much time to spare, though she didn't know what his other plans were or what could possibly be more important than going after violent drug producers. She'd promised to bring her portable GPS so he'd be able to find the exact spot as they'd tagged it.

As near as anyone could tell, someone had broken into the office through the window and deleted the picture files from both the computer and her camera's memory card—someone who'd known about the picture files and who'd known where they'd be.

Peeling back her blanket and sliding into bed, Elise couldn't seem to quiet the voices inside her head that kept shouting out conspiracy theories. Maybe the window hadn't been broken by someone breaking in. Maybe whoever had deleted the files had only broken the window to make it look as though there had been a break-in. Leroy could have done it. He had a red truck, too.

And Leroy hated the McCutcheons. What better way to get back at their old enemy than to frame him for producing drugs? Elise didn't like to think her uncle would do such a thing, but after seeing the way he'd held a gun on Cutch that afternoon in the hangar, she knew his hatred ran deep. Deep enough to frame Cutch? Maybe—though she couldn't imagine her uncle would allow anyone to shoot her out of the sky.

Which left one other possibility: Cutch. She'd seen how quickly he jumped into the conversation, asking her to call Leroy as soon as she'd mentioned to the sheriff that Cutch had been with her when she'd downloaded the photos. He was the one with the tank on his land. He was the one with the suspicious history. And though she wasn't exactly sure how he could have done it without them noticing, there was every possibility he hadn't *found* the broken window at all. In order to divert suspicion from himself, Cutch may have broken the window.

Which would mean she wasn't just cavorting with the enemy. She was cavorting with the man who'd tried to have her killed.

SIX

Exhausted, Elise hit the snooze button too many times the next morning and found herself sneaking into the early church service right after the opening prayer. She ducked into a pew near the rear of the sanctuary, grateful that the Labor Day weekend meant many of the regulars were out of town, so there was still a space big enough for her to squeeze in near the back. From across the sanctuary she caught the eye of her friend Phoebe, who gave her a conspiratorial smile.

Elise immediately wondered what Phoebe knew. Her best friend since kindergarten, Phoebe had been the reason she and Cutch had become involved with one another in the first place. When Phoebe had married Sam Scarth eight summers ago, Elise had been her maid of honor. Since Sam and Cutch were good friends in addition to being first cousins, Cutch had been the best man. He'd simply been too easy to fall for.

Between the couple's shower they'd cohosted and the urgent secret planning meetings they'd held—not so much because they'd needed to, but because they were looking for an excuse to see each other—it hadn't taken long for Elise to fall head over heels.

Looking back, Elise realized part of the problem began

with her father's long-running insistence that she avoid Cutch completely. She'd always been curious about their dark-haired sworn enemy and wondered why he was so terrible. Given her expectations, he'd seemed so much more the opposite of terrible once she'd gotten to know him.

"Love your enemies." Pastor Carmichael's Scripture reading cut through her thoughts, and Elise quickly flipped her Bible open to the passage from Luke chapter six, wondering, as she often had before, how Pastor Carmichael always seemed to know just what to preach about to speak to her heart. Funny thing was, loving her enemy had been what had gotten her into trouble in the first place.

If she hadn't been so enamored with Cutch, she might have been able to see past his charm and good looks. Instead, she'd been delighted with his plan to announce their relationship at Sam and Phoebe's reception. Once the newlywed couple left for their honeymoon, Cutch was going to get up on stage and announce that the long-standing McAlister-McCutcheon feud was over, based on the grounds of their love for one another.

At least, that was the way Cutch had said it would happen. Instead, he'd pulled Elise back behind the stage curtains and planted a kiss on her lips just in time for his young cousins to jerk open the curtains and reveal their private moment in front of everyone. Even as laughter had filled the room, even as Cutch had laughed along with everyone else, Elise had stood there, looking like a total idiot, waiting for him to proclaim his love.

Finally, when the laughter had begun to die down—and she'd looked at him pleadingly—he'd shaken his head and simply said, "I'm sorry. I can't."

She'd been so shocked that she'd barely made it off the stage before bursting into tears. And the worst part? All along, she'd secretly hoped he was planning to propose to her that night. She couldn't have been more wrong.

No, loving her enemy was a bad idea. After what she'd experienced, Elise was that much more curious about what the Bible and Pastor Carmichael had to say on the subject. She was convinced the biblical instructions were correct but couldn't figure out what had gone wrong in her case. She'd loved Cutch. To her shame, she still felt attracted to him.

While the pastor gave examples and told moving stories to elaborate on his message, Elise listened intently and felt her heart softening. She *wanted* to do God's will, to love others and reach out to them, but why did God have to make things so complicated? Surely God didn't really mean for her to love a McCutcheon, did He? She couldn't imagine God would ask her to turn her back on her father and uncle and all the other McAlisters who would probably disown her if she and Cutch got together.

No, loving Cutch would only lead to more division. It would only cause problems and not solve them. In retrospect, she realized Cutch's betrayal eight years before had done her a favor by forcing her out of a relationship that was doomed to failure in the first place. There was no way she and Cutch would ever make a good match—not with the way he kept secrets and especially not after he'd plotted to embarrass her. The fact that their families hated one another only made the reality that much clearer.

Elise looked down at the Bible on her lap. *Love your enemies. Do good to those who hate you.* Her heart felt torn, and she prayed God would help her sort out what she should do—before her heart got broken again.

She still felt conflicted after the worship service when Phoebe met her near the back of the sanctuary.

"I'm surprised to see you here. I thought you'd be leaving to go to that glider festival in Kansas City."

Elise shook her head. "It didn't work out. It's a long story." Which she didn't want to have to explain—at least not until everything was sorted out. There was no sense in making Phoebe worry. She changed the subject. "What are you guys doing this weekend?"

Phoebe's response was suspiciously nonchalant. "We're having a small family barbecue after church. Just me and Sam and the kids." She eyed Elise as she spoke. "Cutch was planning to join us, but he suddenly developed more pressing plans."

Elise tried to keep her expression blank, but her friend pressed on.

"He mentioned doing something with you." Phoebe raised her eyebrows suggestively.

"It's really nothing." Elise moved forward as the milling line of worshippers slowly inched toward the rear doors where Pastor Carmichael chatted with each one in turn as he shook everyone's hands.

"I guess I'm just confused," Phoebe said frankly. "You know, I originally wanted to invite you over to the barbecue, too, but I didn't think I could because Cutch was going to be there, and you always refuse to have anything to do with him. But now the two of you are spending time together—"

"It's not what you think." Elise didn't want her friend getting any wild ideas.

"So you're not going to tell me?" Phoebe looked hurt. She and Elise shared almost everything. Phoebe turned, blocking the rear sanctuary doorway as the rest of the crowd moved through to the atrium without them. "Just like you've never explained what happened after Sam and I left the reception. What did Cutch do that was so bad?"

"I don't want to talk about it." Elise knew Phoebe had heard all about the kiss, but she'd never explained to Phoebe that Cutch had claimed he was going to publicly announce his love that evening. How could she admit to anyone that she'd been foolish enough to fall for the guy who'd only been out to humiliate her?

Phoebe stepped back so they could move forward toward the waiting pastor. "Fine. But do yourself a favor, Elise, and *think* about it, will you? Because I don't think Cutch hates you nearly as much as you hate him."

Elise tried to keep her expression blankly cheerful, but her friend's words hit a soft spot near her heart. Her reaction must have showed on her face, because Phoebe leaned in and added quietly, "In fact, I sometimes think he feels quite differently."

Before Elise could recover enough to ask Phoebe to clarify what she meant, the two caught up to Pastor Carmichael, and Phoebe began asking the minister questions about the morning's message. Elise gave his hand a quick shake and ducked out the door, trying to shove all thoughts of Phoebe's words from her mind. Of course Cutch hated her. Why else would he have been so cruel?

Cutch stopped his truck at the corner at the north end of his property. He could see Elise's little blue Honda topping the next hill. He wondered how the tiny car would do on the soft dirt road that split his property. Not well, he was sure.

He hopped out of his truck and waited as she approached. For a second, he thought she might try to drive right past him, but at the last moment she stopped and rolled her window down.

"Yes?"

"Thought you might want to ride in with me. I have

four-wheel drive." He expected her to make a smart retort and maybe even turn him down flat, so it surprised him when she nervously tucked her hair back behind her ears before agreeing.

"That sounds like a smart idea. Where should I leave my car?"

After helping her find a flat, out-of-the way spot near some bushes along the road, Cutch climbed back in his truck and buckled his seatbelt in wonder. Elise McAlister was sitting in his truck for the second time in two days. He regretted that it had taken such dangerous circumstances to bring them back together. The truck rumbled over the soft loess soil as he made his way down the unfinished road.

They pulled to a stop behind where Sheriff Gideon Bromley leaned against his silver truck, casually dressed in khaki cargo shorts and a dark blue polo shirt instead of his uniform.

"Ready?" he called out as Cutch and Elise hopped out of the truck.

"Are you in a hurry?" Cutch asked.

"The sooner I get out of here, the less chance I'll get in trouble for being late." The sheriff's dark eyes glinted, and he pointed off into the woods. "This way."

Cutch and Elise followed closely. Though he was unsure what the sheriff was worried about getting in trouble for, he could commiserate. Most people feared the sheriff and figured he was above reproach—just like many people were intimidated by Cutch's powers as county assessor. Cutch's job involved determining the value of all the properties within the county, which established their property tax rate. Since he held power over what people paid in taxes, many of the people of Holyoake respected him. Others resented him. He was sure the sheriff was in a similar position because of his power to fine and arrest people.

As they made their way through the grove, Cutch kept his eyes peeled for any sign of the large white tank he'd seen from the sky. Between his familiarity with the land and what he'd observed as they'd circled over in Elise's plane the day before, Cutch could tell when they were closing in on the spot.

As he walked, his sense of foreboding increased. Ever since he'd spotted the tank from the sky, he'd been itching to get a closer look at it. Helping Elise had set him back. The slashed tires and missing photographs had set him back even further, as had going to church that morning. But church and helping others came first—always. Now Cutch feared he was about to pay for that priority.

The hills opened up into a wide valley, and Cutch was certain he recognized the same area where he'd seen the tank. At the same time, Sheriff Bromley came to a stop in front of them. He looked down at the GPS Elise had let him hold, then made a slow circle, looking carefully around the clearing.

"Well," the sheriff said finally, "I don't see anything."

Elise looked over his arm at the GPS unit. "This is the right spot. This is the location we tagged from the sky." She turned to Cutch. "Where's the tank?"

His fears had been realized. The tank was gone. And Elise seemed to think *he* knew something about it. He looked around for some sign of what might have happened. They needed clues—preferably clues that would point away from him as a suspect.

Rutted, disturbed soil caught Cutch's eye, and he stepped past the pair to where broken plants and trampled leaves revealed the fresh presence of some disruptive activity.

"I don't know where they took it, but you can see exactly where it was." He crouched down to get a closer look.

The expression on Elise's face was one of disbelief. "So the tank is gone? Where is it?"

Cutch's eyes followed the wheel ruts that trailed back to join the others on the rough road. "They moved it."

Elise felt fear creeping back over her. She'd seen the anhydrous tank clearly in the pictures Cutch had taken— the pictures that had been erased. Now the tank was gone, too. Obviously the guilty party didn't want any evidence found that could incriminate them. Much as she'd like to believe they'd leave her alone, Elise was afraid they'd go to equal lengths to eliminate any potential witnesses.

Sheriff Bromley crouched next to Cutch and inspected the tracks. Finally he shook his head. "There's nothing here to tell me one way or another what was pulled through here. There's absolutely nothing that links these tracks—or this site—to the tank in the pictures that I have also never seen." He stood. "Is there anything else?"

Realizing the sheriff probably felt as though they'd wasted his time, Elise looked frantically around the valley. Trees and underbrush obscured everything. "Don't you think you ought to do a thorough search? *We* saw it."

The sheriff sighed. "I have no evidence that says any illegal activity took place here. Even if there was an anhydrous tank here, having and transporting the tanks aren't illegal unless they're being used to produce drugs. You claim someone was trespassing on your property, but I don't have any evidence that points to any suspects." He shook his head. "If you turn up anything new, I'll look into it. But there's nothing more to look at here, and right now I have somewhere I need to be."

Cutch stepped closer to the sheriff. "But somebody

shot Elise's glider down out of the sky. She could still be in danger."

Appreciation rose inside Elise at Cutch's words.

The sheriff looked back at Elise. "Do you want me to take a look at your glider?"

She hesitated. What good would that possibly do? He'd see there were holes in it. The holes wouldn't mean anything more than the ruts on the ground. "Do you think it would do any good?"

"I doubt it."

"Then I guess not. Sorry for keeping you."

The sheriff handed back her portable GPS unit and headed off the way they'd come in.

Elise looked down at the GPS in her hands and squeezed her eyes shut as a despairing feeling began to rise inside her. She didn't have anything to prove what she'd been through. The only one who even believed her was Cutch. And that was a very small consolation, indeed.

"Hey." Cutch's hand lightly touched her shoulder. "It's going to be okay."

"Is it?" She looked into his clear blue eyes and tried to find the answers there. Cutch looked like he was just as confused and afraid as she felt.

He dropped his hand. "I don't care what the sheriff said. If somebody was producing meth out here, there's got to be more evidence than just a few ruts in the ground. Want to help me look around?"

After the sheriff's official prognosis, Elise wasn't sure what good it would do, but she also couldn't think of anything that would be more likely to help them. "Sure."

They poked around for quite a while, peeling back leaves, squinting at the ground, scrutinizing the underbrush for signs of human presence. Elise tried to keep a safe distance between her and Cutch. She didn't want to get too close to him.

After a half hour search had turned up only more ruts and trampled places but no clear footprints, Elise gradually wandered farther up the valley, expanding her search area. A chemical odor tickled her nose—something offensive but oddly familiar. Honing in on the smell, she followed the scent around the next hill, rooting among the underbrush for anything that looked out of place. She gasped when she spotted something, and Cutch came running up behind her.

"What is it? Are you okay? Did you find something?"

She let out a slow, disappointed breath. "Never mind. Just a few of those small camping fuel tanks. Somebody must have been camping out here—or at least having a cookout." She reached for the metal container.

Cutch grabbed her hand. "Don't touch them. This is exactly what we're looking for."

"What? A sign that the drugmakers liked to grill out?"

"No. Camping fuel is an ingredient in making meth."

"An ingredient? You mean they use it to cook it?"

"No. I mean it goes into the drug."

Elise was certain she hadn't understood him correctly. "The drug that people put into their bodies has camping fuel in it? People put camping fuel in their bodies?" She expected him to retract his statement once he heard how absurd it sounded.

Instead, Cutch looked at her with a saddened expression. "Why do you think meth is so destructive? All of the ingredients are toxic. This is dirty, disgusting stuff."

Elise shuddered. "Who would do that to themselves?" She couldn't understand. "You'd have to be so messed up."

"Most drug users are," Cutch acknowledged as he poked around under the ground cover near where she'd found the camping fuel container. After a moment, he sucked in a sharp breath. "Empty blister packs," he muttered. "Stripped battery casings."

"More signs of meth?" Elise asked, wondering how Cutch knew so much about what went into making the drug. Her earlier doubts about his involvement resurfaced.

"Exactly." He turned and looked back at her, a disgusted look on his face. "That's it. I'm calling the sheriff and telling him to come right back out here. I don't care what his plans are."

Elise nodded. She wasn't going to interrupt him before he called the sheriff, but she made a mental note to ask him how he knew so much about meth production. "I'll get a lock on this spot with my GPS." She pulled out the device and pushed a sequence of buttons. "We've moved far enough down the valley. It could be tricky finding this place again otherwise."

"Good idea," Cutch agreed as he flipped open his phone. Before he began to dial, a slamming sound echoed through the pecan grove. Cutch froze.

Elise met his eyes as the fear leaped back into her veins. Another slamming sound quickly followed the first. It sounded like car doors. And if she had to guess, she'd say the noise originated from back near where they'd left Cutch's truck. She recalled hearing the distant sound of an engine running only moments before, but she hadn't paid much attention, having assumed the noise was coming from the road. Obviously, she'd been wrong.

Quietly, Cutch stepped closer to her and placed one hand on her arm. He mouthed "shh" silently.

He needn't have bothered. Elise wasn't about to make a sound. Something told her that her life depended on it.

Indistinct men's voices pierced the otherwise-silent woods.

Cutch bent down and whispered in her ear. "They're between us and the truck. Let's head for the north road. Quietly."

Crouching low in an attempt to maximize the cover from the underbrush, they picked their way silently in the direction away from where they'd parked Cutch's truck. The voices seemed to follow them as they rounded the curve of the next hill. When they ducked behind the solid trunk of a pecan tree, Elise whispered to Cutch, "Do you think it might just be the sheriff? Maybe he changed his mind and came back."

Cutch shook his head slightly, the small movement causing his nose to brush her cheek as she leaned close to stay within whisper range. Her heart beat hard—not just from fear but from his unwelcome proximity.

"He seemed pretty eager to get out of here. Besides, it sounds to me like there are two or three of them."

Elise silently shushed him as the men drew close enough for their voices to be heard again. "Can you tell what they're doing?"

"No. I'm going to try to take a look." Cutch leaned around the tree. When he ducked back, he pressed his lips to her ear and whispered almost silently, "They're looking for something. Maybe they came out to finish cleaning up the drug site."

Elise ignored the delighted shiver that ran through her at the touch of his lips against her skin. Their circumstances were serious. She had to stay focused. "But they've got to know we're out here. They had to have seen your truck."

A rough man's voice sounded far too close, interrupting their thoughts. "Maybe they're not out here."

Another harsh voice responded, "Of course they're out

here. Do you think they left the truck and walked out?" The man spoke with an odd lisp.

"They could have had a problem with flat tires." The words came out with snide laughter. Elise wasn't sure if it was a third voice or the first speaker answering back. Either way, she knew these were the guys who'd slashed Cutch's tires the night before. They may have even slashed his tires again.

Cutch's lips brushed her ear once more. "They're getting too close. We've got to get out of here."

Elise pulled back just far enough to look into his eyes. "But they'll see us," she whispered.

"At least we might have a chance of getting away," he whispered back, his nose buried in her hair where it fell across her temple. "The hill curves around from here. If we can make it another ten yards, we should be able to get past their line of sight."

Elise didn't even realize she'd taken hold of his arms until she became aware of the death grip she had on his shirtsleeves. His muscles rippled with movement under her fingers, and she felt comforted by his strength, especially since her life was now in his hands. "Wait until their backs are turned."

Peeking narrowly past the tree that hid them, Cutch held her arms as tightly as she held his. "They're moving away," he whispered silently without so much as glancing back. "When I say go." His hand tensed on her arm.

A moment later, with a slight nod, Cutch whispered, "Let's go. This way."

Having already looked over their intended route, Elise took her first few steps silently, moving as quickly as she dared and keeping low.

They brushed past some leaves, and she flinched, wondering if the men behind them had heard the noise. With fear prodding her, she moved faster.

The curve of the hill was riddled with saplings and bushes. They darted through, trying to find the clearest route while at the same time trying to be quick about it.

More leaves brushed against them. A stick cracked below Cutch's foot, its sound like a tiny gunshot to Elise's ears, though fortunately the men behind them were talking again and gave no indication of having heard it.

They were all but around the hill. Elise felt like lunging herself forward like a baseball player diving into home plate, but she forced herself to keep her eyes open and move quietly. Cutch held her hand tightly in his as they scrambled through the clear spots. They were more or less around the hill when a deer startled and jumped out of the bushes in front of them.

Elise gasped.

"What was that?" the rough voice carried clearly from just around the hill.

"It's just a deer."

"Who do you think spooked the deer? This way!"

As soon as she heard the men take off in their direction, Elise ran with abandon, tearing loudly through the underbrush beside Cutch, whose full-bent dash made just as much noise. But it didn't matter anymore how loud they were. They *had* to keep their lead over their pursuers.

"Over here," Cutch whispered, tugging her straight down the next valley.

She followed as quickly as she could run, but protested, "This is a straight shot. They'll see us."

"Just trust me," Cutch hissed back.

As the valley opened up, Cutch veered off along the north side. At first Elise thought he was running without a particular direction in mind, but a moment later, she saw the faded wood sides of a small old building, a crescent moon cut into the door.

An outhouse.

Cutch towed her toward it. "In here." He opened the door, and they both nearly fell inside, letting the door close behind them.

The weathered little shed was full of cobwebs. Elise looked down through the light that streamed in through slits under the eaves to see a fat spider on her arm. She suppressed a scream and flicked it off. Quickly she took in her surroundings.

For an outhouse, it was a good-sized building, with a bench occupying the rear half of the shed and two hinged lids evenly spaced on the bench. A two-seater, as the old-timers would say.

While sounds of their pursuers echoed through the woods outside, Cutch lifted the bench. "Down."

"What?" Elise gasped as quietly as she could in her surprise. "In the pit?"

"Nobody's used this thing in decades, if ever."

Elise peeked into the dark hole and then looked back up at Cutch. She couldn't do it.

"I see footprints! They went this way!" The voices sounded even closer than before.

"I'll go first," Cutch offered, "but you've got to come down after me."

She could hear the men crashing through the under-brush outside. It wouldn't be long before they noticed the outhouse.

Cutch leaned the whole bench back and jumped in feet-first. Elise heard his feet thump against the hard dirt floor of the pit. Looking up at her from just below the rim, he whispered intently, "Hurry!"

At the same time, Elise heard a man's voice shout

outside, "Look over there! Do you think they went in the outhouse?"

She was trapped, with no choice but to stay put and wait to be found or to drop inside the latrine pit and pray they didn't think to look there. She scrambled into the hole as fast as she could and felt Cutch's strong hands holding her securely around her waist as she let go of the rim above them and her feet dropped to the hard earth.

Cutch pulled the bench shut above their heads.

The loud blast of a shotgun startled her, and she clung to Cutch at the sound of the wood above them splintering, raining down debris onto the seats above their heads. They ducked a little lower in the pit, which was no more than six feet deep, if that.

"Oh, Dear Lord," she prayed in a whisper, hardly aware that she'd instinctively pressed her face into Cutch's strong shoulder. He wrapped his arms protectively around her.

"Lord, keep us safe." Cutch's quiet prayer was barely audible over the sound of the next blast.

The sliver of light that shimmered through the slit between the seat and the lid seemed to grow a little brighter. Elise wondered if the men were planning to blast the little outhouse to bits.

Another gunshot sounded, and more debris rained down.

"That ought to do it," a vengeful voice announced.

Cutch's voice whispered close to her ear. "Let's get down as low as we can. Stay silent. Maybe in the dark they won't be able to see us even if they look under the lid."

With all the holes the gunmen had punched in the dilapidated outhouse, Elise figured there would be plenty of light available. But after all the shots they'd fired, they'd have at least obscured any telltale fingerprints she and Cutch may have made on the dusty bench above them.

She and Cutch flattened themselves into cramped sitting positions on the dirt floor of the hole, with their backs pressed tight against the sides. Elise leaned against his shoulder, and his arm held her protectively.

Normally she would have pushed him away. But normally, she wouldn't be hanging out in a latrine pit. At least it didn't seem to have ever been used. The inside was dry and smelled of damp earth.

Elise squinted up at Cutch. She couldn't see his face in the darkness. She prayed he would be equally difficult to see if the men above them thought to look under the seats.

As the door above creaked open, Cutch's arms tightened around her. Elise didn't dare breathe. She huddled against Cutch and prayed. If the man shot them where they were, their bodies would never be found. And even if by some odd chance their bodies were recovered, she knew her father would never get over it if she was discovered dead in a latrine pit, shot while in the arms of a McCutcheon.

SEVEN

"Empty!" The lisping voice shouted, disappointment resonating through that lone word.

"They must have gone up the hill."

"No, down the valley. It'd be easier going there."

"What do you say we split up?"

"Okay, but let's hurry! We're wasting time."

The door slammed shut above them, dimming what light seeped through. Elise sagged as she let out a slow, silent breath. She could still hear the men's voices, but the sound quickly faded as the men outside crashed away through the woods, their words once again becoming less distinct as they increased the distance between them.

"Thank you, God," Elise finally prayed when she was fairly certain they were out of hearing distance.

"Amen," Cutch concurred, relaxing his hold on her but not removing his arm from around her shoulder. "That was a close call."

"Too close," Elise agreed, shuddering to think how narrowly they'd escaped. "How did you know this outhouse was here?"

"It's my land, isn't it?"

"I suppose so," Elise acknowledged, feeling frustrated, as she always had been when Cutch refused to give her a straight answer. It was one of the many reasons why she knew a relationship between them would be doomed to disaster, regardless of whatever else he'd done to her. The man was far too secretive.

But Cutch seemed to pick up on her tone, and his voice softened. "This was the outhouse from our homestead. My grandfather moved it out here when the main house got indoor plumbing. But I don't think it actually saw any use here."

"See, that wasn't so difficult, was it?" Elise snapped as her impatience with Cutch clashed with the unwanted attraction she felt toward him. Her nerves were already thin from their frantic dash through the woods.

Cutch remained silent, but his arms tensed behind her. Had she made him angry? She tried to tell herself she didn't care if she had, though if she was honest with herself she had to admit she cared deeply about his feelings. But she wasn't going to get anywhere worrying about Cutch's feelings. There were far more pressing issues to discuss.

"Who do you think those men were? That guy with the lisp sounded awfully familiar."

"You're right. I'm trying to place where I've heard that voice. Seems to me it's a guy who's missing some teeth."

"But not an old guy." Elise searched her mental records for the elusive memory. "Donnie Clark!" she whispered with assurance, finally placing it. "Uncle Leroy hired him to help out at the airstrip several years ago. He's one of the few people with a pilot's license in this county, but he wasn't there long."

"That's right. He's never stayed in any job for long." Cutch sounded thoughtful. "Probably for the same reason he lost his teeth so young."

"Why do you suppose that is?"

"Meth." Cutch's voice echoed through the pit with certainty.

"Meth makes people lose their teeth?" Elise grew more disgusted with the drug every time she learned something new about it.

"Sadly, yes. And if he's addicted to the drug, it's no wonder he'd do anything to maintain his supply—including doing dirty work for his supplier."

The authority behind Cutch's words sparked the curiosity Elise had felt earlier. "How do you know so much about meth?"

Warm breath tickled her ear as Cutch sighed beside her. "It's a long story."

"I've got time. I'm not planning on showing my face out there until those goons are long gone. The last thing I want to do is poke my head out and get it shot off."

She could sense Cutch's struggle as he wrestled with her question.

Irked by his reluctance to share, she leaned away from him, as though to look him in the face if there had been enough light to see him. "Why can't you just tell me? Is it that difficult to be honest with other people?"

Cutch squeezed his eyes shut against Elise's probing questions. His instinct was to put her off, to make some half-related remark that would distract her just enough so he could change the subject while at the same time hopefully making her feel as though they'd dealt with her concerns. It was a trick he'd honed over the years, which he'd learned from his father and used successfully throughout his life whenever people's questions cut too close to his dreams that he wanted to protect from the criticisms of the outside world.

Too bad the trick wouldn't work with Elise. She saw

right past his evasive answers. When he'd first gotten to know her eight years ago, her insight into his true motives had impressed him until she'd started getting too close. He'd learned to hide his secrets more carefully around her. But as his father had learned when death had crept close, some secrets didn't need to be kept from everyone. Could he trust Elise with his whole messy past? She might hate him if she really knew.

But she already hated him.

So maybe he had nothing to lose.

"My grandfather," he began slowly, "was a meth addict."

It took a moment for Elise to respond. "When? I thought he died a long time ago. And meth is a newer drug."

Cutch almost felt glad she knew so little about the drug. She was still innocent as far as that was concerned. His knowledge weighed on him. "Its popularity is newer, but it's been around since World War II. According to what I was able to learn about it, the Nazis gave out the stuff to help their soldiers fight beyond the natural boundaries of exhaustion. It gave them a temporary advantage over the enemy. And if it eventually destroyed the person, well, they didn't care."

"Oh my."

"I don't know how my grandfather stumbled into using it. He was a fighter pilot in the war. Somewhere along the line, either he decided or someone decided for him that he ought to have every advantage the Nazis had."

"Even if it destroyed him," Elise concluded.

"Yes." Cutch sighed. "Grandpa came back from war a drug addict. His boyhood dream was to transform these useless hills into the world's foremost pecan-growing region. The idea itself is a good one. He just didn't have his head on straight and planted the trees too close together.

The trees only produce nuts on their outermost branches, but if the trees are too close to other trees, those branches don't get enough sunlight."

"And the trees don't produce any nuts," Elise finished for him.

Cutch nodded, the movement rocking her head gently where she'd placed it against his shoulder in the darkness. "I've tried clearing out trees, with some success, but the mature trees already have their growth ends developed, so I'll never get full production out of them. There are some pruning tricks I've tried that have helped some, but I doubt they'll ever have the kind of yield they could have if they'd been planted correctly to begin with."

"Then how will you ever make it work?"

"I've cleared forty acres and planted it with new stock—spaced correctly. The trees take at least six years to reach productive age, though, so this fall's harvest will be the first indication I'll have as to whether the plan will work. Eventually, I'd like to come back through here, sell all the old trees for wood and replant the whole section."

"That's a lot of work."

"I know. But I want my grandfather's dream to come true. He lived out the end of his life as a bum and died thinking he'd been a failure. My father became a workaholic to overcome that stigma."

"I guess I didn't realize." Elise's words were soft. She paused. "So, that explains the connection to the drug, but I guess I still don't see why you know how it's made."

Cutch shrugged. "When I found out what my grandfather had been addicted to, I wanted to know more. I did some research, but there's not a lot of information out there. The antidrug laws have really cracked down because they don't want people to know how to make the stuff."

"Makes sense."

"I did some Internet searches on the subject, little knowing the authorities can and do monitor such activity. The FBI red flags searches for things like methamphetamine production, and when they get repeated hits from the same user, they contact the local authorities to investigate. It didn't take long for the sheriff to show up—"

"They arrested you because of an Internet search?" Elise interrupted.

"I was never arrested," Cutch corrected her. "But I was a person of interest, and you can believe they investigated me thoroughly. Because of that history, I'd guess if they come up with anything new to link me to the drug, they're not going to care if I was considered innocent—" Cutch broke off, listening.

Elise tensed in his arms as the sound of distant men's voices echoed through the woods once again. "They're coming back," she whispered.

"Let's pray they don't find us." Cutch said, scooping her smaller hands into his large ones before beginning a whispered prayer.

"Please God," Elise chimed in, "please keep us safe. And help us to bring whoever's after us to justice. Amen."

Cutch kept his eyes pinched tightly closed as he waited, tense arms wrapped around Elise, until the voices drifted off in the direction they'd come. From what he could tell, Donnie and his pals were probably headed back toward his truck. As vengeful laughter faded away, Cutch recognized its source.

"Did you hear that guy who keeps laughing?" he asked Elise.

"Yes, it gives me the creeps—like he's taking pleasure in hunting us down."

"It sounds like Darrel Stillwater."

"That's right. He and Donnie are always getting in trouble together. I suppose he uses meth, too," Elise said.

"I wouldn't be surprised. I wish I knew who they were working for, though." Cutch couldn't recall hearing anything about where either of the men were working in recent months.

Once the woods had been silent for long enough that the birds had started chirping again, Elise suggested, "We should get out of here."

"I don't know. I'm not convinced they're gone. Like you said before, I don't want to stick my head up only to have it blown off. Besides, the way they talked about my truck and flat tires, I'd guess I'm going to have to give Gary's Garage another call."

"You might be right," Elise acknowledged, slumping against him defeatedly. "How do they keep finding us out here?"

Cutch fought back the urge to stroke her hair back from her face. He wanted so much to comfort her. Instead, he felt certain his words would only disturb her that much more. "I don't think it's a coincidence."

"I was afraid of that. Their timing has been too good. So who do you think is really behind all this?"

"I don't know who Darrel and Donnie are working for these days," Cutch admitted, "but it's got to be someone with connections, someone with inside information. With the timing on all this…think about who knew we were out here. Think about who knew we were going after those pictures last night."

Elise shuddered. "The sheriff?"

Cutch hated to agree with her. "He's the most obvious choice. And remember when you first called him to say your glider had been shot down out of the sky—he didn't offer to come right out then. That just doesn't seem right."

"I don't want to believe he'd be in on this. We need his help. I always thought he seemed like a trustworthy man."

"But if he's not the one behind all this, who else could be?"

Fear churned inside Elise. An hour before, she'd have considered Cutch a suspect, too. But after the way the men had shot at both of them, she didn't really see how he could be—not unless his own men had turned on him.

Which left one last option—one she liked even less than the others. Her voice sounded hollow when she offered her suggestion in the darkness of the latrine pit. "Uncle Leroy."

Cutch stiffened beside her. "Your uncle? I know he pulled a gun on me yesterday, but he wouldn't try to shoot you down, would he? You're his niece. And you work for him."

"I know." The sigh that escaped her mouth sounded shaky. "I always thought we got along just fine, even though he's not what you'd call an affectionate person. But he *hates* you, Cutch. He hates all the McCutcheons. I saw that when I looked down that gun barrel yesterday. He hates you enough he didn't even lower the gun when I stepped in front of it." Her voice cracked.

Cutch pulled her closer against him.

As much as she wanted to push him away, she'd been through too much over the last two days. His strength was the one comfort she had left. She leaned her head against his shoulder as she continued. "Uncle Leroy drives a red truck, and Donnie Clark has worked for him before. Leroy knew where we were headed when we left with the ladder yesterday, so he could have slashed your tires and deleted the pictures. Maybe he even broke the window to make it look like an outside job."

"But he didn't know you'd be out here today," Cutch noted.

"No," Elise admitted, "but he could guess you would be. He might have sent those guys out here after you, not realizing I'd be with you." Her voice dropped to an empty whisper. "Or not caring if I was."

Elise's heart clenched, surprising her with how much her uncle's possible betrayal hurt. Hadn't she learned when she was six years old that she couldn't trust anyone—not even her own mother? How had she let herself become so secure around her uncle? She knew better. And she knew better than to cozy up to Cutch, too.

Slowly, she pushed away from him and raised herself on trembling legs. "We've given them enough time. We should get out of here before those guys come back and decide to check this outhouse again."

Cutch stood beside her, stretching up his long arms to raise the hinged bench above their heads. "Want me to go up first? That way, if anybody gets their head shot off—"

"Don't talk like that!" Elise chided him in a whisper.

"You're the one who said it the first time."

"But that was my head I was talking about then," she corrected him.

Cutch turned to face her in the dim light. "I'd have thought you'd be glad to have the world rid of another McCutcheon."

Elise looked up into his eyes and saw him gauging her reaction. She tucked her hair absently back behind her ears and fought back the affection she felt for him. Affection like that would get her nowhere. She couldn't trust her mother; she couldn't trust her uncle. Why would she even consider trusting a man who'd already betrayed her?

Love your enemies. The words from the morning church service surfaced in her mind. But it was that kind of love that got Jesus killed. Elise set her lips in a firm scowl. "I don't want you getting shot when I'm with you. Then they'd find me for sure," she stated boldly, hating herself when she saw disappointment flash across Cutch's eyes.

"Fine," he said flatly. "You want to go first?"

"I'd love to."

Elise stepped up on Cutch's bent knee, grabbed the edge of the enclosure above her and then stepped onto his bowed shoulders. A moment later she stood inside the shot-up outhouse.

"How are you going to get up?" she asked, looking down at him.

"Stand back."

Elise did as she was told, cracking the door open and standing in the doorway. She watched in wonder as Cutch grasped the aging wood and muscled himself up from the hole. He was a strong man—strong and independent.

"Now what?" she asked quietly when he stood beside her. "To your truck or to the road?"

"Those guys came in near my truck. If we head that way, we might find them waiting for us. And besides, if they slashed my tires again, the truck won't do us any good."

"So, the road then?"

"I guess so."

They made their way quietly northward.

After some trudging, Elise asked quietly, "Do you think they slashed my tires, too?"

"I hope not. We'll need your car to get us out of here. If those guys drove in on the south road, which seems likely, then there's a good chance they don't realize where your car is parked. The sheriff saw you arrive in my truck. If he's the one behind all this, he would have passed that information along to them when he told them to come after us out here." They reached the fence line and clambered through the thick brambles.

Cutch held down the barbed wire for her to climb over. He stepped over after her and met her at the side of the road, his eyes scanning the trees and hilltops. From where they stood, autumn-red sumac camouflaged their position while allowing them to see a wide swath of the surrounding area.

Elise watched Cutch's eyes as he scrutinized their surroundings, presumably for any sign of the gunmen. She took in the determined set of his jaw and the weathered care lines that had begun to form around his eyes since she'd last known him. He'd aged well. She wondered how such an attractive, godly man had made it almost to his thirties without marrying, but she couldn't possibly ask him without feeling as though she was expressing some sort of interest in him.

And she wasn't interested. Not in Henry McCutcheon IV.

When Cutch glanced over at her a moment later, she realized with embarrassment that he'd caught her staring. She felt even more mortified as her cheeks burned a bright red, essentially giving away the fact that she knew she'd been caught looking at him. Hurrying toward where her car sat parked in the distance, she quickly circled around and verified that her tires had not been tampered with.

"Thank goodness." She sighed as she climbed behind the wheel.

"Amen to that. I'm done playing in the woods."

"Do you want me to try to drive you to your truck?"

Cutch folded his body into the small space of her passenger seat. "Please, no. This car will get stuck before we get halfway there, and then we'll really be sitting ducks. Can you take me to Gary's Garage? He can help me."

Though she pointed the car toward town, Elise protested, "But it's Sunday. Gary's Garage is closed. Maybe I can help you change your tires."

"I don't want to take up any more of your time or put you in any more danger. If I can find Gary, he won't be shy about billing me extra for making him work on a Sunday."

Elise smiled. To be honest, she didn't feel comfortable spending any more time around Cutch than she already had—especially after the close quarters they'd shared while hiding from the gunmen and the way he'd caught her staring at him. "Thank you."

"It's not a problem."

Fortunately, Gary's Garage was on the edge of town, so Elise didn't have to endure the embarrassment of being seen with Cutch by the entire town of Holyoake. Gary's house sat next door to his business. Elise waited patiently while Cutch went up to the porch and rang the bell. When Gary answered the door, Cutch spoke with the man a moment before turning and waving her off.

Elise was glad to go. If nothing else, she needed to rinse off the feel of the dirt and the bugs she'd spent the afternoon keeping company with. And maybe, if she was really lucky, she'd be able to wash away the feeling of being close to Cutch.

When she arrived home, she was glad to see that her father wasn't around. She knew he worried about her, and if he saw how bedraggled she looked after her run through the woods, he'd no doubt worry that much more. After a quick shower and change of clothes, she felt significantly better, though her heart still hammered uncomfortably and she found herself jumping at her own shadow. Being shot at so many times would do that, she figured.

There wasn't much to eat in the fridge, and Elise recalled with disappointment that she'd left the lasagna at the airfield office. She needed to finish it up in the next couple of days.

Recalling that the sheriff had promised to have the airfield computer returned as soon as their expert had finished trying to retrieve the picture files, she decided to head over there and see if she couldn't make some headway on the pictures she'd taken of the Mitchum's corn maze so she could deliver their final product to them. After all, she still had a business to run. No way would she allow the gunmen to destroy her livelihood, too.

As she pulled into the airfield parking lot, Elise noticed a familiar red truck parked in front of the office. It was not Uncle Leroy's but Rodney Miller's. Glad she didn't have to face her uncle, Elise let herself in to find Rodney seated in front of the returned computer. The small-framed older man enjoyed the same kinds of computer games as the teenagers she knew, but he quickly closed his program when she entered the office.

"Hi, Elise," he greeted her. "The sheriff brought the computer back. I thought they might have messed stuff up, but it all still seems to work." He finished with a characteristic nervous laugh.

Elise smiled patiently. "Glad to hear it. Do you mind if I retrieve the pictures I took of the Mitchum's corn maze? They were erased from my camera, so the only copies I have are on that computer."

"Help yourself. I should probably head out." Rodney hopped up and shuffled past her to the door.

After locking the door after him, Elise sat down at

the computer and tried to convince herself she had no reason to feel uneasy. Whoever was after her had destroyed whatever evidence she might have had against them. They didn't need to come after her, even though she was in a place where they'd broken in before. And she was alone. And it would soon be dark.

Shaking off the nervous chill she felt, Elise switched on the radio, which was tuned to the nearest Christian radio station, and cranked the volume high enough to drown out her fears. The praise music that filled the room made her feel a little better.

To her relief, the corn maze pictures were all still saved on the hard drive, and she started to load them onto a portable drive, though the large files and aging computer made the process a slow one. While she waited for the first files to load, she checked her e-mail and was cheered to find messages from several of her friends expressing disappointment that she wouldn't be joining them at the Labor Day Powered Glider Festival.

Distracted by the messages, she'd almost forgotten about how vulnerable she was, alone in the little building that had been broken into before, when she heard a noise above the sound of the radio. She switched off the music just in time to hear the locked doorknob rattling as someone tried to open it. Then she heard a solid thump as though the person on the other side had thrown the weight of their body against the door.

EIGHT

The smoldering anxiousness she'd been feeling burst into flames of fear. Elise glanced over at the window. Someone, probably Uncle Leroy, had taped clear plastic across the opening. That wouldn't stop an intruder.

The door rattled again, and Elise looked around the small office, trying to think of what she could use as a weapon to defend herself.

"Elise? Are you in there?" Cutch's voice called from the other side of the door.

Hurrying to open the door, Elise didn't try to mask her relief. "Oh, Cutch. You scared me half out of my wits!"

"Are you okay? Why didn't you answer when I knocked?"

The sound of his voice hit her burning fear like a splash of cool water, and she stepped back into the room, making way for him to follow after her. "Yes. I'm okay." The hitch of a terrified sob broke through her words, but she bit it back. "I didn't hear you knocking. I was listening to the radio."

"It's okay." Cutch settled a comforting hand on her shoulder. "I didn't mean to frighten you. I saw your car parked here as I was driving past, and I didn't like the idea that you were here alone. I was only going to check on you, but then when you didn't answer the door—" his voice faded, and he looked a little sheepish "—I thought maybe something had happened to you."

An odd, tender feeling swirled in her heart at Cutch's protective words, but Elise chose to ignore it. Since she hadn't spoken to him since leaving him at Gary's Garage, she asked, "How were your tires?"

"Slashed."

"All four?"

"Yes. They finished the job this time."

"Anything else?"

"Nothing that I've found. These guys obviously want us to know they know who we are. They're trying to scare us, that's all."

"Well, it's working. I'm scared," Elise admitted, hugging herself. "Did you call the sheriff about your tires?"

Cutch made a strained face, "I don't think we can trust him, but at the same time, if he's in on this, I don't know what I can possibly gain by not telling him, since he'd know about it already. That might just make him more suspicious. So, I went ahead and reported the camping fuel tanks and other debris we found, too. If nothing else, I'm doing my part by being forthcoming about what I've found."

"I think that's wise," Elise assured him. "Even if the sheriff is involved—and I still hope he's not—we've got to do the right thing and trust that justice will be served." She met his eyes. He looked so uneasy, and she realized he probably felt the same way about the situation as she did. Though she didn't want anything else connecting her to him, it was still a comfort to know she wasn't alone.

His grateful smile told her he appreciated her understanding. "Were you planning to stay out here by yourself much longer?"

After the scare she'd had when Cutch had arrived, Elise gave an involuntary shudder that shook her whole body. "I don't plan to. But I need to finish downloading the pictures of the corn maze, and I was hungry…." Recalling how he'd enjoyed the lasagna the day before, and realizing she still had several pictures to download, she asked, "Have you had supper?"

Cutch was glad Elise made good lasagna and that she was willing to share it with him. If that was the only thing he had to be glad about after all the rotten things that had happened that day, then he was determined to focus on that blessing.

While Elise pulled out the pan of leftover lasagna, Cutch casually scrolled through the pictures of the corn maze on the computer. "You're a really great photographer," he observed.

Elise laughed from the kitchenette area a few feet away. "Can I quote you on that for a brochure? Maybe it would help drum up business."

Cutch turned toward her. "Are you hurting for customers?"

"I could always use more." Her tone sounded light-hearted as she scooped lasagna onto plates to reheat.

"You know, I was thinking that I'd love to hire you."

"Really? What's the project?"

"I could use your help with the county assessments. Every time someone's property increases or decreases in value, it should affect their tax rate. But sometimes I don't find out about these things for years. Did you know Rodney Miller's barn burned to the ground three years ago? He's been paying taxes on that thing, and it hasn't even been there. But if I could fly over the county a few times a year,

I could spot major property value changes without having to wait to hear about it through the grapevine."

Elise looked intrigued. "I didn't know about Rodney's barn, and he even works for Leroy. You'd think he'd report it so his taxes would go down."

"He claimed he never thought about it." Cutch shrugged. "But he's far from the only one. People love to make improvements on their properties without reporting them. Bruce Bromley built several outbuildings and an inground swimming pool. I was finally tipped off about it a few months ago. He claimed the work had just been completed, but some of that stuff had to be a few years old, at least."

Setting the timer on the microwave, Elise shook her head. "He's the sheriff's brother. You'd think he'd know better."

"People will do whatever they think they can get away with. And trust me, Bruce Bromley's property taxes went up considerably. Since I can't prove those improvements weren't there in previous years, he's saved himself a bundle on the past few years' taxes," Cutch noted. "That's why I think it might be helpful to fly over the county on a regular basis. Bruce is far from the only person who's put in buildings of late, and Rodney's probably not the only guy who's been overpaying. I'm familiar enough with the land that I should be able to spot changes from the sky."

"We could probably work something out," Elise offered agreeably.

"That would make my life easier," Cutch said, turning back to the corn maze pictures on the computer while Elise monitored the reheating lasagna. He scrolled through the shots of the labyrinthine cornfield and gave a low whistle. "This is quite the maze the Mitchums have this year."

Elise came up behind him. "Pretty amazing, isn't

it?" she said, tracing a path over the screen with her fingernail.

"There's a pattern to it," Cutch noted, letting his index finger hover above the screen near hers. "Three right turns, three left turns, two right turns, two left turns,"

"One right, one left, then back to three again," Elise finished. "Mr. Mitchum told me he likes to keep to a formula when he cuts out the path that leads through the maze to the other side. Then he comes back through and puts in all the dead ends."

"So there's only one way out of the maze?"

"Only one. There's a playground at the end to reward the children who make it through." Elise traced the path, her fingers skirting close to his. "A person could spend hours in there looking for the right path. If you didn't know the formula, you might never find it."

He closed his fingers around her small hand.

She looked up into his eyes. "Cutch," she chided him softly, but he heard the question in her voice, the faint undertone of possibility that gave him hope. Or tormented him for no reason.

His heart squeezed out a prayer for help as he risked telling Elise, "I want to be friends."

"What?" Her words were soft, but she pulled her hand away.

He let her go. "When this is all over, when these guys are caught, I don't want to go back to never talking to you again. I want to be friends."

Elise turned her back on him and tended to the lasagna.

For a moment as he watched her check to make sure the lasagna was heated through, he wondered if she wasn't about to rescind her supper invitation. Maybe he should have kept their small talk light and kept his hands to

HOW TO VALIDATE YOUR
EDITOR'S FREE GIFTS!
"THANK YOU"

1. Peel off the FREE GIFTS SEAL from front cover. Place it in the space provided at right. This automatically entitles you to receive two free books and two exciting surprise gifts.

2. Send back this card and you'll get 2 Love Inspired® Suspense books. These books have a combined cover price of $11.00 for regular-print or $12.50 for larger-print in the U.S. or $13.00 for regular-print or $14.50 for larger-print in Canada, but they are yours to keep absolutely FREE!

3. There's no catch. You're under no obligation to buy anything. We charge nothing—ZERO—for your first shipment. And you don't have to make any minimum number of purchases—not even one!

4. We call this line Love Inspired Suspense because every month you'll receive books that are filled with inspirational suspense. These tales of intrigue and romance feature Christian characters facing challenges to their faith and lives! You'll like the convenience of getting them delivered to your home well before they are in stores. And you'll love our discount prices, too!

5. We hope that after receiving your free books you'll want to remain a subscriber. But the choice is yours—to continue or cancel, anytime at all! So why not take us up on our invitation, with no risk of any kind. You'll be glad you did!

6. And remember...just for validating your Editor's Free Gifts Offer, we'll send you 2 books and 2 gifts, *ABSOLUTELY FREE!*

YOURS FREE!
We'll send you two fabulous surprise gifts (worth about $10) absolutely FREE, simply for accepting our no-risk offer!

Steeple Hill®

(LISUS-EC-10R)

himself, but he was tired of the wall that stood between them. He felt as though he had to open up the lines of communication, even if it meant risking getting thrown out by Elise. He waited for her verdict, fully expecting her to order him away.

Instead, she carried the plates to the small table with her lips pinched shut. She settled the plates on the table and looked up at him with a frustrated expression. "Why would I be crazy enough to trust you again?" she asked, pulling her chair roughly out from the table and sitting down. "You proved to me eight years ago—" her voice caught and she folded her hands over the lasagna.

"Can I bless it?" he asked tentatively, sitting down across from her.

"Fine."

As Cutch asked a blessing over the food, he felt the weight of the decision he'd made eight years ago—the promise he'd made to his father and what had resulted because of that promise. He wished he could go back and do things differently, but he didn't know what he would change. He'd done his best.

He looked up, expecting to find her glaring at him, but instead her eyes brimmed with tears. His heart twisted a little more. If he hadn't already felt guilty for what had transpired between them, he would have started to then. Instead, he just felt that much worse. There had to be a way to make things right with Elise. But how?

Elise had already started in silently on her lasagna. The lump in his throat told Cutch he wouldn't be able to swallow anything until he'd tried to make amends.

"Eight years ago at Sam and Phoebe's wedding reception," he stated slowly.

Before he got any further, Elise jumped up and turned her back on him again. "I need a drink," she muttered, pulling out a glass and filling it with water at the sink. "Would you like some water?"

"Yes, please."

Elise shoved the filled glass toward him, and the water sloshed toward the rim.

"Thank you."

With a shrug, Elise sat opposite him. She picked up her fork and started cutting into her lasagna with force. The noodles were no match for her angry dicing.

Cutch knew he needed to say something to make things right between them, to soothe her injured heart, but he couldn't think what that would be. Words caught in his throat. "I'm sorry," he said, at a loss. "I'm sorry for what happened at the reception."

The fork fell from Elise's trembling hand and clattered against the table. She didn't pick it up but instead reached for a napkin, which she knotted in her hands. "Are you? Are you really? Because let me tell you how it came across from my perspective. You *said* you were going to announce our relationship to everyone. It was *your* idea, Cutch. I didn't put you up to it. You told me you wanted to end the feud with our—" she choked, and the word came out as a whisper "—love."

"I was going to."

"Then why didn't you?" Elise backed her chair away and threw her hands into the air. "It was a setup—the whole time. You didn't care for me. You intentionally made me believe there was something between us so you could get me up on that stage and kiss me in front of everybody, in a deliberate plot to humiliate me and the whole McAlister clan in front of the entire town of Holyoake."

It hadn't been the entire town of Holyoake, but Cutch figured that was a moot point. Their dearest friends and relatives had all been there. "It was never my intention to embarrass you."

"Then what was your intention? If you really were going to announce our relationship, you missed your shot."

"I know." Cutch could feel her torment and wished there was something he could do to relieve it, but he was still bound by his promise to his father. Until the older man died or freed him from his vow, he couldn't tell Elise what had motivated his actions. And without that critical bit of explanation, none of the rest of what he'd done would ever make sense to her.

There was a conversation he desperately needed to have—but not with Elise. Not yet. He finished his lasagna silently and then pushed away from the table. "Thanks for supper," he said. "I don't want to leave you here alone."

Elise looked over at the computer. "It's okay. My pictures are done downloading." She'd finished her lasagna as well. "We can go."

While Elise grabbed her portable hard drive and shut down the computer, Cutch stood in the doorway, waiting and watching her.

"I'm sorry," he said again, as she came to a stop next to him in the doorway.

Elise shrugged off his apology. "Forget about it." Her eyes lingered on his, sparking torturous hope. "I don't want to think about the past anymore. We have enough trouble to deal with."

"It's okay," he assured her, wishing he could pull her into his arms but certain she'd only push him away again—and rightfully so. But he couldn't leave her so melancholy. "God knows what's going on. We just have to trust Him."

"I trust God," Elise assured him as she stepped past him through the door. "I just don't trust whoever's been after us." She locked the door behind them and hurried to her car.

As Cutch watched her leave, he felt a small part of his heart go with her. The promise he'd made to his father had stolen too much from him. Eight years ago, he'd been forced to choose between his love for his father and his love for Elise. They'd been so young, and their relationship so new that at the time he couldn't justify turning his back on his dying father in favor of a relationship that might not ever get off the ground.

But his father had fought the cancer off—twice. And Cutch's love for Elise had never gone away. Though he'd told himself for years that he'd made the right decision, lately, every time he saw the woman he loved, he wondered if he hadn't made the wrong choice. If so, there was only one way to make things right.

He had to talk to his dad. Though he feared the emotional discussion might be difficult for his father given his fragile condition, he couldn't let the old man die without at least trying to clear things up from the tangled way they now stood. As Elise's taillights disappeared, Cutch climbed into his truck and prayed.

"Lord, I need your help. I need to talk to my father, but I don't want anyone to get hurt." He looked up into the darkening sky. Menacing clouds swirled ominously in the distance. "Amen."

NINE

Elise woke up in pain. She'd tossed and turned all night, her dreams haunted by gunshots and fear. Now her legs throbbed from their desperate flight through the woods and the cramped quarters of the latrine pit. She winced when she attempted to stand. Though high school cross-country had been years before, she still recalled that the best way to get rid of the pain was to get out and run again. With a grimace, she dug her sneakers out from under her bed.

When she stepped out the back door of the farmhouse, the scent of rain and early autumn filled her nostrils, and she took a deep breath. Late summer was fading quickly, and the rain that had fallen overnight had brought down the first of the yellowing leaves, covering the farmyard in a sodden carpet of gold. A hazy mist hovered near the tree line, and even the sun seemed reluctant to rise.

Elise smiled. If she had to run, she was at least glad to do so in her favorite kind of weather.

The gravel crunched under her running shoes as she headed off down the road, hobbled by her pain but determined to stretch out her stride and force the burning acid from her muscles. Early morning birdsong filled the air, lifting her spirits.

By the end of the first mile, Elise felt like she was going to crumple into a ball. She considered heading back, maybe even at a walk, but she refused to give the men who'd chased her the day before even that small victory. Instead of turning home, she pressed on down the road, realizing only after the intersection was long behind her that she'd pointed herself on a direct course toward the McCutcheon farm.

Whatever. She wasn't afraid of the McCutcheons.

Her legs were screaming by the time she came up on the windbreak that circled the McCutcheon home. Though the farm had once filled an entire section, Elise had heard that Cutch's grandfather had sold off all but the house and surrounding acreage after he'd lost his pecan grove. The McCutcheons still lived in the house, though Cutch's dad had spent a thirty-year career at the First Bank of Holyoake and had never shown any interest in farming.

Elise had never been to Cutch's boyhood home. From what she understood, he still lived with his parents. She tried to tell herself she ought to think less of him for that, but she honestly found it sweet that he'd moved back to help take care of them. There'd been some rumor that his father wasn't well, but Elise didn't like to listen to gossip—especially gossip about McCutcheons, and she had no idea how much of what was whispered in town was true.

In response to the cries from her throbbing muscles, Elise slowed her pace as she came up toward the house. She'd driven by it only a couple of times over the years; even though it was close to the McAlister farm, she tended to plan her routes around it. McCutcheons, she'd found, were best avoided.

Wet leaves clung to her sneakers, threatening to make her slip. She stopped and flicked them off her feet before glancing up. The gracious gabled dormers of the third floor peeked above the trees in front of her. It was a lovely house, really.

Elise picked her way across the leaves toward where the lilac bushes that rimmed the windbreak put on their last sparse show of late summer flowers. She wondered if Cutch had arrived home safely the night before. She knew it wasn't any of her business, but she peeked around the bushes and felt relieved when she saw his truck, new tires gleaming, parked in front of the garage.

She blinked. The farmstead was spotless, with hanging baskets of red geraniums highlighting the wide front porch and cheerful mums showing off from the beds around the foundation. An old windmill's blades were held hostage by magenta-and-white clematis, while flowers of the same colors curled around the mailbox by the road. In all, it was a charming picture—one that made her wonder how anyone who lived in such a precious place could really be as evil as the McCutcheons were supposed to be.

Reaching toward a branch that obscured her view, she bent it back, looking closer, her mind filled with questions and wonder. How often as a child had she tried to imagine how the awful McCutcheons must live? She'd pictured them reigning over a mud-caked yard with angry dogs chained about, but this was nothing like that. An orange-and-white kitten hopped down from the porch steps, pouncing on a sleepy grasshopper.

Elise stifled a giggle.

"Ever wonder what terrible kind of people must live there?"

Startled by the deep voice behind her, Elise spun around to see Cutch approaching her from the road. She could feel her face turn scarlet, and she tried desperately to think of some excuse as to why she'd be peeking through his bushes. "I-I was just—"

"Spying?" Cutch offered, crossing his arms across his sweat-drenched T-shirt. He'd obviously been out for a run, as well, though from the looks of it he'd made it farther than she had. "I suppose it's understandable. There are rumors I might be involved with making drugs, and a person can't be too careful these days. And you never can trust a McCutcheon."

She felt wrenched by his words, especially when she saw the pain behind his eyes. Okay, so she was mostly guilty of thinking those things. "I was just out for a run," she faltered.

"Want to come inside?" Cutch's offer surprised her. "Check things out? I can even let you search the barns. I promise you, Elise, I have nothing to hide from you."

"Oh, really?" He might have had a point about the spying, but his antagonizing words were more than she would stand there and take. She crossed her arms and faced him in a posture identical to his. "Then why don't you ever give me straight answers when I ask you questions?" Granted, he'd shared a little with her the day before when they'd been hiding out, but that had been the first time ever. And he'd practically run away rather than answer her questions the evening before.

His tired eyes winced slightly, and Elise knew her words had hit home.

"You want answers?" He stepped closer to her and cupped her elbow with one hand. "Come on."

Startled, Elise thought about fighting him, but she didn't nearly have it in her. And besides, she *was* curious to see the inside.

They stepped past the frolicking kitten and made their way up the front porch steps. The front door turned smoothly on its hinges, and Cutch led her into the open front room, where houseplants bloomed amidst antique wooden furniture and lace curtains let in plenty of light through the broad picture windows. Framed photographs of a younger Cutch and his little sister Ginny were clustered around Hummel figurines on the crocheted piano runner.

Though the farmhouse wasn't fancy, the place was a lot cozier than the home she'd grown up in. But then, her father wasn't much of a decorator.

Cutch kept to the braided rugs as they crossed the gleaming wood floor and made their way through the dining room to the kitchen. "Can I get you something to drink?" Cutch asked quietly as he opened the fridge. "I've got orange juice, tea, milk. My mother has some grapefruit juice in there, but I've never been convinced that's potable." He looked up at her with a drawn expression, but she caught a faint twinkle behind his eyes.

Elise rubbed her arms, feeling really, really stupid for spying on Cutch's house and getting caught and now for being dragged through her "investigation" by a man who was so cordial, so charming.

He brushed his hands back through his sweaty hair, leaving it standing at odd angles.

So cute.

"Water's fine."

He nodded and set about pouring her a glass. "Have you had breakfast?"

She shook her head.

Cutch handed her the glass of water before pulling a carton of buttermilk from the fridge. "You like pancakes?"

Thirsty, Elise took a long drink before answering. Was Cutch going to make her pancakes? From scratch? "You're not thinking of cooking me breakfast, are you?" she asked.

Lifting out a package of bacon, Cutch met her eyes over the fridge door. "I thought that would be the civilized thing to do. But since I'm a McCutcheon, maybe I don't understand how these things work." He set a carton of eggs next to the bacon on the spotless counter.

The tearing in her heart was more than just guilt, especially after the verbal jabs she'd thrown his way. She fidgeted with her hair, but it was already tucked behind her ears, and no amount of retucking was going to make her feel any better. "Maybe I should just go."

Cutch had her shoulders in his hands before she finished her sentence. "Elise, it's okay. I'm not mad at you. Just let me make breakfast, and then I'll give you those straight answers you've been looking for."

Answers? She could hardly believe it. But then, she could hardly think at all. Cutch was standing way too close. And no guy had any right to look so good in a sweaty T-shirt with a day's worth of stubble on his chin. She looked at the ingredients he'd set on the counter. "Are you going to cook the pancakes in the bacon grease?"

"That's the way I like them." The twinkle returned to his eyes.

Elise felt herself smiling, though she told herself she knew better than to get her hopes up. "The higher they fly, the harder they fall" was another one of her father's aphorisms. "Can I help you with anything?"

Cutch told himself not to get his hopes up. Just because Elise stood next to him tending the bacon while he stirred the pancake batter didn't mean they wouldn't be fighting again in a minute. But it felt so right to work next to her in the kitchen. They worked in contented silence except for a couple of questions, like when she wanted to know how he liked his bacon or when he asked if she preferred her pancakes thicker or thinner.

They both liked crispy bacon and thick silver-dollar cakes.

Maybe McCutcheons and McAlisters weren't so different after all.

And, overly optimistic as it may seem, he wondered if it wasn't more than just a coincidence that Elise had appeared at the farmstead mere hours after Cutch had finally broached the crucial subject with his father. Their conversation the evening before had been a long and difficult one. Out of respect for his father's delicate condition, Cutch had finally left the issue unresolved, but he felt optimistic about the progress they'd made.

He'd just flipped the first batch of pancakes when he heard his mother's distinctive footsteps in the hallway above them, headed for the stairs. A moment later, Anita McCutcheon stepped into the kitchen and gasped.

"Oh!" She threw her hands into the air like he hadn't seen her do since his father had been cleared of cancer the first time. This was a good sign.

He glanced over at Elise. She looked scared.

His mother made a beeline for Elise and wrapped her in her ample embrace. "Oh, praise the Lord, praise the Lord!" She cupped Elise's face in her hands and pranced in place. "I have prayed for this day!" She gave her another hug.

Elise looked over his mother's shoulder at him. Her expression said *help*.

He grinned back at her and continued flipping the pancakes.

"Oh, how I've prayed for reconciliation between our families," his mom went on, squeezing Elise's cheeks.

"And God is good. God is *so* good. He brought you here." Her voice caught. "Just in time," she whispered.

Cutch looked up to see tears forming in his mother's eyes. They both knew his father only had a few more weeks, at best. Was there still time to work things out before he died? Cutch looked back at Elise. Her eyes were full of questions.

"Want to join us for breakfast, Mom?"

"No. I've already eaten. But I tell you what. I'll get your father up and dressed. And then maybe he'd like to join you for breakfast." Anita gave Elise another squeeze. "Oh, God is good," she said, patting Elise's forehead a couple of times before she hurried back up the stairs.

Cutch grinned at Elise. She looked a little dazed but not upset.

"Breakfast is ready," he informed her with a smile.

Elise couldn't recall when she'd ever had a breakfast that tasted so good. She looked around the cozy kitchen as they ate at the worn oak table and wondered how she could feel so at home in her enemy's house. She was more at home than she often felt in her own house, especially after the grilling her father had given her when she'd arrived home the night before. He was worried about her, and she couldn't blame him for that. She just wished he'd stop being so overprotective.

Cutch ate in companionable silence opposite her. She was on her second pancake and he on his third when she heard the floorboards creaking above them, and soon after, she heard a shuffling on the stairs.

It had been years since Elise had seen Henry McCutcheon III, or Old Cutch, as everyone in Holyoake referred to Cutch's dad. Still, she couldn't believe how much he'd changed. Gone was the powerful stature, the stout figure, the thick salt-and-pepper hair. The man who made his way toward the table looked thin and frail, with faint wisps of white hair swaying across his otherwise bald head.

She'd spent all of her life fearing this man. Now she wondered what she could possibly do to help as Cutch jumped up to assist his father into a chair. Apparently the rumors about his poor health were more than true.

As Cutch fixed his father a plate, Old Cutch reached across the table and patted Elise's free hand where it rested near her napkin. She looked up into his clear blue eyes.

Even his voice sounded weak as he asked her slowly, "How do you feel about my son?"

Elise didn't know how to respond. She looked at Cutch for guidance. His wide eyes met hers as he set a plate in front of his father. "Dad, I don't think—" he began.

But Old Cutch cut him off. "It's okay, son. I want to hear what she has to say." He turned his attention back to Elise. "You can think about your answer for a minute." He folded his hands over the steaming food and mumbled a few words of thanks before digging in.

Still unsure what to say, Elise finished her second pancake slowly and tried to think. What were the McCutcheons up to this time? Was it another trick? If she claimed to have feelings for Cutch, would his father use that information to embarrass her again?

"Well?" the old man prompted as he finished off his pancake.

Elise gave him the most honest answer she could. "He makes me angrier than anyone I've ever met."

Both men startled a little at her response, and Old Cutch gave a weak chuckle. "Well then," he mused, looking pleased. "Is that the truth, is it?"

"Yes, sir."

"And how do you suppose he feels about you?"

Elise looked to Cutch, but he turned away and carried their dishes to the sink. While Elise was still struggling with what to say, her cell phone rang from the pocket of her windbreaker. Old Cutch nodded at her to take the call. Wondering who could be calling so early in the morning on the Labor Day holiday, she answered it quickly.

"Elise? I need your help," Uncle Leroy said. "Rodney didn't show up to work today."

TEN

Cutch tried not to listen in on Elise's phone conversation, but he could clearly hear her uncle Leroy's gruff voice carrying over the phone. He had a crop dusting job for her—one that had to be done that morning, before the heat of the day sent the pesky grasshoppers deep under the canopy of leaves, shielding them from the insecticide she would spray. Cutch understood how these things worked. Elise had to hurry.

But he had to talk to her, too. His father's line of questioning had clearly shaken her. Even if he couldn't explain everything, he had to at least try. He couldn't let her walk away from him again.

"I have to go," she informed him as she closed her phone. "Thanks for the breakfast."

"I want to come with you," Cutch offered.

Elise froze. She opened her mouth, and he knew a refusal was on the tip of her tongue.

"You'll need a ride anyway, unless you plan on jogging back to your car." He watched the truth of his words sink in and mustered up the courage to take a step closer to her. Dropping his voice, he explained, "Besides, I still owe you some answers."

Hope filled him as she looked him full in the face. She

didn't smile, but she didn't frown, either. "I'd appreciate that. But we have to hurry."

"Just let me grab my jacket."

"I'll wait outside."

Cutch ran to the hall closet for his windbreaker, knowing that the cool morning would seem even colder once they were flying through the sky. As he darted for the back door, his father intercepted him.

"Tell her," Henry McCutcheon's firm voice belied his frail condition.

"But last night, you said—"

His father cut him off. "It's time."

Cutch didn't know what to make of that but nodded and headed for the door. Elise was waiting for him. She climbed into the truck, and he tried to sort out where to start—eight years of secrets and misunderstandings spread backward in a tangled time line. He grasped for a thread. "My father has cancer," he announced as he put the truck into gear.

"I wondered," Elise buckled her seatbelt. "Is he doing all right with it?"

"He's in home hospice care."

Elise looked at him. Cutch would have liked to return her gaze but felt he should keep his eyes on the road. "That means he's not going to get better."

"I'm sorry. I didn't know."

"Nobody knows—no one except the doctors and nurses in Omaha. Dad hides out at home and hasn't let us tell anyone."

"So, why are you telling me?"

Cutch took the corner for the airfield, warring inside on what to say. There was so much more he needed to explain, but he knew Elise would need to focus her full attention on her flying, and their conversation was sure to be more than distracting. It would be unfair to her and even unsafe to distract her with any more information now. "It's time," he answered with the words his father had given him, the only explanation he had. Until Elise finished spraying the field, that would have to be enough.

Twenty minutes later, they were in the sky with the load of spray Leroy had prepped for them. The cockpit noise inside the yellow two-seater plane made it impossible for Cutch to say any more to Elise; besides, he wanted her to be able to focus on what she was doing. Crop dusting was dangerous work, and a single miscalculation could bring the plane down. Even good pilots died that way, including Elise's own grandfather. Cutch's respect for Elise soared as she maneuvered the plane through a series of tight turns just above the tops of the plants.

"Done?" he asked as she brought the plane up at the end of the field.

"Done with that one," she explained. "Unless Uncle Leroy has another job for me. I wonder if he was able to get in touch with Rodney."

"That man worries me. What do you think he's up to?"

"Rodney? I can't say, but I agree with you. He drives a red truck, and I can't understand why he wouldn't tell anyone about his barn burning down unless he was trying to hide something. And now he's disappeared?"

Cutch felt relieved that Elise agreed with him on his suspicions regarding her coworker. "We could swing by and see what he's up to. I know where he lives." As county assessor, Cutch knew where everyone lived—or at least where they owned property.

"Excellent idea," Elise agreed, shifting their course in

the open airspace. "I know where his place is, too. And if he asks later, we'll tell him it's a courtesy wake-up call."

"True enough," Cutch agreed. If the man was innocent, he might as well get back to work so Elise wouldn't have to take up the slack. And if he was guilty, they needed to know. He watched out the window as they headed north toward the old Miller farmstead. Like many of the smaller Loess Hills farming operations, the Millers hadn't been able to make a steady go of farming and had sold off much of their land over the years. Now Rodney lived alone in the old farmhouse at the northern end of the county. Cutch hadn't realized before how close the place was to his pecan grove.

Suspiciously close.

He kept his eyes trained on the familiar checkerboard of fields below them as they left the flatter, more fertile land of the Nishnabotna River valley and neared the Miller place in the hills. The loud cockpit muffled outside noises, so Cutch didn't notice the approaching plane until it entered his peripheral vision.

"Elise, watch out! There's a plane on your left!"

His stomach dipped as Elise pulled the little yellow duster high up out of the path of the passing plane. It swept past below them, creating turbulence in the air with its disturbing bulk.

"What was that?" Elise asked as she glanced back in the direction the plane had gone.

Cutch craned his neck to see through the narrow windows of the tiny cockpit. The larger blue-and-white plane made a wide arc behind them. "They're coming back around!"

Elise gunned the engine and took them low this time, angling to her right. Cutch couldn't see the oncoming plane as well from that position, but he knew Elise could. They skirted the topmost branches of the windbreak below, and Cutch braced himself as the bully plane swept near. He was sure they were headed for a direct hit.

But Elise followed the tree line as it dipped away. The windows rattled as the bigger plane buzzed by, landing gear all but grazing them as Elise flew the duster dangerously close to the ground.

"Try to get an ID on that blue jay," Elise said as she pulled the duster back up. Then she got on her radio, "Sky Belle to Big Bird. Sky Belle to Big Bird."

Frustrated, Cutch tried to get a closer look at the plane while Elise quizzed her uncle on who might be sharing the airspace with them. Leroy didn't know anything about the larger plane.

Nor could Cutch make out any sort of identification mark other than the decorative blue swish along the white sides of the plane and some pinkish-red smudges on the underbelly.

"Got anything?" Elise asked him.

"Nothing I can see clearly. If you could get a little closer—"

"I'm trying to get *away!*"

"Good luck with that. He's coming around again."

They were above the Loess Hills by this point, and Elise kept the plane low above a tree-topped ridge. They were in a dangerous position with nowhere to go, but Cutch understood Elise's strategy. The bigger plane was faster and more powerful than their little crop duster. But between Elise's flying skill and the small size of the yellow bird they flew in, she far outranked the bulky blue jay in maneuverability. And the Loess Hills gave her something to maneuver through.

"Hold on to your breakfast," Elise warned him. "This could get a little dippy."

"Uh, Elise," Cutch began slowly, gripping the sides of his seat as he stared down the approaching plane. "I know you need to concentrate, but I think you should know that they've got a gun."

No sooner had he spoken than the sickening sound of crunching aluminum shuddered through the small craft.

"Where are we hit?" Elise asked, zigzagging the little yellow plane through the hills.

"Can't be anything too important," Cutch assessed, given the way Elise was able to steer the plane so agilely. The other plane was flying well above them, and Cutch craned to see through the narrow windows. He caught enough of a glimpse of the underbelly of the plane flying above them to see clearly what the pinkish smudges were that he'd noticed earlier.

Red mud.

Not a particularly common soil type in southwest Iowa, though he knew he'd seen it once or twice during his assessment inspections. But where? It was difficult to think when he was being shot at.

Thunk! Thunk! A couple more bullets sank through their aluminum.

"I'm losing integrity on my right wing." Elise sounded angry as she brought the plane up. "I can't risk flying through these hills when I don't know how my plane is going to respond." She got back on her radio. "Big Bird, this is Sky Belle. I don't know how much longer I can stay aloft. They're shooting—" *Thunk!* "I'm going to try to land her." *Thunk! Thunk!* Elise flinched visibly as more bullets tore through the fragile plane. She rattled off their coordinates to her uncle.

"There's a good flat stretch of road up here by the corn maze if you can make it that far," Cutch observed, trying to be helpful.

"I don't want to lure them to a place where there are innocent people," Elise protested.

"There's no sign of anyone at the maze," Cutch countered. "I don't think they open until later." In spite of all they'd experienced that morning, it still wasn't even nine o'clock.

"Okay then." Elise sounded relieved as she steered them back toward the flat lands of the river valley that began just a few hilltops away. The plane began to chug. "*If* we can make it that far." She didn't want to slam into a steep hillside. With a few final sputters and burps, the engine gave out, and Elise glided the wounded plane toward the road. It didn't look like they were going to make it.

"Try to get past the hills," Cutch encouraged her.

"I can't," she said, pulling up on the controls with little response. "I've dropped below critical speed. The plane's not moving fast enough for me to control it." Her voice dipped to a whisper. "Lord God, I could *really* use some lift right now."

The bully plane, so much faster in spite of its greater bulk, flew past them, shaking the air around them and sucking them along in its wake.

"Thank you," Elise whispered as the plane lifted higher in the wake of the larger plane—just high enough to keep from slamming into the side of the hill. "Now's my shot." She tensed as the wheels bumped the gravel on the cusp of the last rise before the Loess Hills gave way to the relatively level farm ground where Mitchum's corn maze was located.

The plane sped along the empty road, quickly exhausting its momentum as the larger plane above them came swooping back their way. Cutch opened his door.

"What are you doing?" Elise shrieked.

"Getting out. We stay in here and we're sitting ducks."

"Where are you going to go?"

"The corn maze."

Elise didn't protest as Cutch grabbed her hand and pulled her out the door of the still slowly moving plane. They hit the ground running, and Cutch threw his arm up in front of his face as he crashed headlong into the thick corn at the side of the maze just as the plane above them swooped past, guns firing, kicking up gravel at their heels.

"Get down!" Cutch cried as soon as they'd made it several rows deep into the field.

He didn't have to ask twice. Elise threw herself to the ground and pressed her cheek to the dirt. Cutch flung himself down in the next row and reached between the stalks to cover her head with his arm. "They shouldn't be able to see us."

"True," Elise acknowledged, "but that won't stop them from shooting the field up. Our odds still aren't very good."

Though he didn't like her prognosis, Cutch had to admit Elise had a point. He could hear the plane coming closer and knew it was entirely possible they could be shot at any moment.

"We've got to get out of here!" he shouted over the noise of the close-flying plane.

"But where can we go?" The thwacking sound of bullets hitting corn a few rows over nearly obscured her words. The plane flew past them, leaving them as-yet unscathed.

Elise's question was a good one. If they tried to make a run for it through the corn, they'd be clearly visible from the sky. As long as the plane continued to fly overhead, they had to lay low and pray for the best.

The sound of the plane's engine died away.

"Where are they?" he asked Elise, certain their pursuers wouldn't give up and leave that easily.

"Shh," she responded, shaking her head at him and staring up through the broad green leaves.

Cutch fell silent. The corn field was quiet. He could no longer hear the plane.

"They're on the ground," Elise whispered.

As she spoke, muffled voices carried through the field. "They ran in over here somewhere. Come on. It shouldn't take us long to find them."

Hauling Elise to her feet, Cutch pulled her along beside him as he dashed through the field. "We've got to get out of here. Help me find the path," he whispered as he crashed through the eight-foot-tall corn, the rough leaves scratching against his arms and face.

"They'll hear us," Elise whispered back as she hurried after him, resisting as he pulled on her hand.

"We don't have any choice," he muttered under his breath. "If we can find the path of the maze, we can move quickly and quietly."

"Then we need to go this way," Elise tugged him toward their left.

Convinced she was right, Cutch kept up with her. "That long stretch should be right up here. Then we'll have an easy go of it." He paused a moment, catching his breath, and made eye contact with Elise. They could hear indistinct shouting that sounded eerily similar to the voices that had pursued them through the woods the day before. There was Donnie's lisp and Darrel's ominous laughter.

One harsh voice rose above the others. "They should be right up here!"

Cutch watched Elise's eyes widen as it became apparent their pursuers were right on their tails. Pulling her along, Cutch tore off down the long, straight stretch. "We've just got to stay ahead of them," he whispered.

"And their bullets," Elise whispered back. "Corn doesn't make a very good shield."

"But it does make good cover," Cutch noted as he darted down a side path.

Elise froze and hissed at him. "Not that way. The walls aren't thick enough—they can see straight between the paths there!"

"I know," he winked at her, and he pulled off the bright red windbreaker he'd thrown on for their flight through the cool Iowa sky. He hung the jacket on a couple of sturdy-looking ears of corn and spread out the sleeves to increase its visibility. Then he darted back to Elise, grabbed her hand and headed off in the opposite direction.

They put a couple more turns between them and their pursuers before they heard the gunmen exclaim loudly. Cutch pulled Elise down to the ground beside him as the men began shooting. Though he knew they were a good distance ahead of them, a hundred rows of corn wouldn't stop a bullet. Cutch didn't want to think how many holes they'd likely put in the lightweight jacket. "That should distract them for a minute," he observed quietly.

"It's a good strategy," Elise admitted as the shooting ended, replaced by angry shouts. "And I think I can find another spot where it might work." She rolled to her feet and took off down a long spur.

Cutch raced after her until they came around a bend, and Elise pulled off her own jacket, dressing the corn before hastily taking off the other way. They ran quickly, trying to keep ahead of both the gunmen and any possible bullet trajectories that might result from their shooting.

Finally they came to a three-way turn, and Elise bent double, grabbing her knees and panting. "I already had a workout this morning," she whispered, shaking her head.

Cutch was about to reply when the sound of gunfire echoed through the field. A sharp stinging sensation hit his upper arm followed by a warm trickle down toward his elbow. He lunged at Elise. "Hurry!"

She took off beside him but asked, "Do you think they're that close?"

"Close enough," Cutch observed, feeling the spot on his bicep where the bullet had grazed him. "They just nicked my arm."

Elise knew she shouldn't stop running, but the sound of firing guns had stopped again, so she slowed down enough to look at Cutch's arm while she stumbled forward. "Nicked?" She protested. "Cutch, that looks bad. You're bleeding all over the place."

"Great. All we need is a trail of blood for them to follow." He grimaced, causing Elise to suspect he was in more pain than he wanted to admit.

Wishing she hadn't already taken off her jacket, Elise tried to think of something they could use to stop the bleeding. "We need a tourniquet."

"Let's just get to the end of the maze. Maybe then we can find a better place to hide. This corn doesn't make a very good shield."

"There's that playground where the maze ends. It has a tunnel made of tractor tires. They might not be bulletproof, but they'll give us a lot more protection than this corn." She doubted the old tractor tires would stop the gunmen for long. Hopefully, their pursuers would get stuck in the complex maze.

They dashed through the cornfield as quickly as they could with Cutch holding his arm and Elise trying to force her burning muscles to keep running. She was so glad they knew the formula the Mitchums had used to carve out the trail that led through the maze. Given that advantage, they were able to navigate almost flawlessly through the rest of the complicated maze. From the sound of it, their pursuers weren't having such an easy time.

In her exhaustion, Elise kept stumbling on the old corn roots that jutted up throughout the path. Even Cutch tripped up a few times as he ran awkwardly with one blood-covered hand gripping his arm. Finally Elise spotted the treetops of the windbreak that rimmed the north edge of the field, and a moment later the path opened wide before them.

Cutch ducked toward the entrance of the tractor tire tunnel.

"Wait." Elise stopped him. "That's the first place they'll look. Let's stay on the outside where we'll at least have a shot of getting away if they find us." She was exhausted from running, and much as she'd have liked to head off down the road to where her pursuers would never find her, there was no way her burning legs could carry her much farther.

They hurried around to the far side of the tunnel and ducked behind it with their backs to the tires. They were still exposed on one side, but outside of the tunnel they at least had enough light that Elise could try to inspect Cutch's injury.

"Can I take a look at that?"

Cutch shook his head. "The bleeding's starting to slow down. If I pull my hand away, it will only start up again."

"Okay," Elise agreed, feeling futile that she wasn't able

to help him. She hunkered down next to him and listened. From the sound of it, their pursuers were still a long ways off in the maze and seemed to be quite frustrated. The occasional blast of a shotgun made Elise jump.

"How long do you think we've got?" she asked in a whisper, drawing her face close to Cutch's ear so he could hear her even though she kept her voice low.

"I don't know, but I want to tell you something."

Cutch turned to face her, the tip of his nose all-but-brushing her cheek as he bent close to whisper. "I know I'm guilty of keeping secrets from you, Elise, but I don't want to allow anything to come between us anymore. Maybe McCutcheons and McAlisters can never be friends, but I want to at least try before I give up. You mean too much to me. I can't just walk away."

Elise's throat went dry. *Love your enemies.* The words from the Bible echoed through her mind again. She swallowed hard. McAlisters and McCutcheons had always been opposed to one another, like darkness opposed light and good opposed evil. Except neither of them was evil. And neither of them was truly good, either. They were both guilty of perpetuating the feud.

Her certainty faltered. She knew better than to trust a McCutcheon, but maybe Cutch wasn't out to trick her this time. His clear blue eyes begged for understanding.

The sound of a plane flying overhead pulled her attention away from her discussion with Cutch. Had their pursuers given up and taken to the air again? She couldn't imagine they'd made their way out of the field again that quickly.

She looked up but couldn't see the plane she heard flying low somewhere above them. Shifting away from Cutch, she started to pull herself to her feet to get a better look.

"Stay down," Cutch insisted. "If they decided to get back in the plane to spot us from the air, then we need to get inside the tire tunnel. We're too exposed out here."

Elise clamped her hand onto his shoulder. "It's my plane," she whispered.

"What? They got that crop duster to fly again? I thought the engine was shot out."

"No." Elise shook her head. "It's my Cessna. Can't you hear it?" She poked her head up and looked around, then plopped down next to him excitedly. "I saw it! It's my Cessna."

"Who's in it?"

"I don't know. Maybe Uncle Leroy's coming to help us."

Worry crossed Cutch's face. "But he knows I'm with you. What if it's Rodney? He could be the one behind all this."

"Then we could be in trouble. We need to pray." She cupped her hands gently over where Cutch still had his hand clamped over the wound on his arm. "Lord, please keep us safe," she began, then broke off, listening quietly for a moment and, hearing nothing but the buzz of the plane somewhere in the airspace around them, picking up the prayer where she'd left off.

As they prayed, she felt peace wash over her. After what seemed like much too long, she heard the sound of another engine starting up, and moments later, the big blue-and-white plane flashed by across her field of vision, its red-mud-caked underside clearly visible from below. Elise shrank back against the tires behind her, but the plane was headed away from them. She let out a sigh of relief.

Her cell phone began to chirp.

"I almost forgot I brought this with me." Elise pulled

the slender phone from the pocket of her shorts and met Cutch's eyes over the caller ID screen. "It's Leroy."

"Answer it."

Cutch listened as Elise told her uncle where they were, and moments later her Cessna landed on the gravel road beside the windbreak that shielded the playground. They hurried through a gap in the trees just as Leroy McAlister climbed out of the plane.

"Thanks for rescuing us, Uncle Leroy." Elise ran to her uncle and gave him a hug.

Cutch tried not to feel too jealous. After all, Leroy had chased the gunmen away.

"You get a good look at that plane?" Leroy asked.

"Yeah. And the mud on the bottom. There's only one place in this county with soil like that." Cutch started to explain when Elise interrupted him.

"Cutch was shot in the arm," she informed her uncle, and Cutch recalled that the older man was a trained EMT. "Can you take a look at it?"

As much as Cutch wanted to pursue the men who'd been firing on them, he realized Elise was probably being smart to ask her uncle to look at his arm. He wouldn't get far if he was badly wounded.

"Let me get the first aid kit." Leroy rummaged around in the plane before producing a cross-emblazoned kit. He snapped on rubber gloves and inspected the wound.

Fortunately, Leroy's assessment of the injury was that it was relatively mild.

"Probably just bled so much because you were running. When the blood is really pumping through your veins, things bleed more. If you take it easy, a good butterfly bandage ought to hold it." As he spoke, he squeezed a packet of antibiotic ointment over the spot, which, true to his evaluation, had already stopped bleeding.

As Cutch watched Leroy carefully apply a bandage over his wound, he heard approaching sirens.

"I wonder what those are all about," Elise voiced the same question he'd been thinking.

Leroy chuckled. "I guess they're a little late, but when you radioed to tell me the trouble you were having with that plane, I called 911. Still, there should be plenty for them to draw up a report about."

Cutch swallowed back his protest, realizing it probably wouldn't do him any good at this point, since the sheriff's car was already pulling to a stop just shy of where Leroy had landed the Cessna. Sheriff Gideon Bromley stepped from the driver's seat, his obsidian eyes pinned on Cutch. Deputy Bernie Gills stepped out of the second cruiser.

If he'd thought he could get away by making a run through the maze, Cutch might have tried it. But he was outnumbered and outmaneuvered. Though Leroy had apparently called the authorities with pure intentions, Cutch realized he was in deep trouble.

Because he'd finally remembered where he'd seen that red soil before, and there was an airstrip on that property. The plane that had just attacked theirs had taken off from Bruce Bromley's land.

So it didn't really surprise him when Bruce's little brother approached him and said, "Henry McCutcheon, you're under arrest for the production of methamphetamine."

ELEVEN

Elise gasped and watched in surprise as Deputy Bernie Gills stepped past the sheriff and cuffed Cutch's wrists behind his back. "You have the right to remain silent. Anything you say can and will be used against you." Bernie's voice faded as he led Cutch toward his patrol car.

Elise practically leaped in front of the sheriff. "Why are you arresting him? *We're* the ones who were being chased by a plane! Cutch is injured."

Gideon Bromley turned to her with sad eyes. "I don't really have much choice. We found production materials on his land—with his fingerprints on them. And he's been a person of interest before."

"But *he's* the one who reported finding that stuff out there. Why would he do that if he was guilty?" The story didn't fit. Cutch hadn't touched any of the stuff they'd found on the ground. How would his fingerprints get on it? She knew the sheriff had taken their fingerprints the other night at the airfield office, but his prints shouldn't have matched anything on the evidence they'd found in the woods.

"Maybe it was an attempt to draw suspicion away from himself," the sheriff theorized. "Look, I don't want to have to arrest him, but there's circumstantial evidence, too.

We've had a growing meth problem in Holyoake County for the past six years or so. And for the past six years, Cutch has been buying land—hundreds of thousands of dollars worth of land. Where do you suppose he got the money to do that? The county assessor doesn't make near that kind of salary." Gideon sighed. "The evidence is stacked against him. Pure and simple."

Elise backed away and stood by her uncle, watching with despair as Bernie and another officer drove off with Cutch in the backseat of the cruiser. Where had he gotten the money? She felt desperation rising inside her. She couldn't let them arrest Cutch—not when he'd been about to open up to her for the first time. "What about bail? Can I bail him out?" She had no idea how bail worked. She'd never known anyone who'd been arrested before.

The sheriff shook his head sadly. "Bail for producing meth is one hundred thousand dollars. You'd have to put up ten percent—that's ten thousand dollars you'd never see again."

She'd saved more than that for a new plane. She had the money. "I'll pay it."

"*Cash.* Not a check, not a credit card," Gideon Bromley specified. "And you'd have to put up collateral for the rest. Property. Something worth ninety thousand. So if he fails to make his court appointments, you'd lose that, too."

Elise felt her stomach sink. She didn't have anything worth near ninety thousand—not even if she added up her car and her plane and all her cameras together. "I—I don't have that much."

"I wouldn't expect you to put up that kind of money for a McCutcheon, anyway. Everyone knows your families can't stand one another." The sheriff shrugged. "You had an incident you wanted to report?"

Though everything in her wanted to run after Cutch,

Elise figured the smart thing to do was to tell the sheriff what had happened and pray he'd sort it out. Surely if Cutch was innocent they wouldn't be able to keep him for long. While she explained everything to the sheriff, her mind swirled with questions.

Where *did* Cutch get the money to buy his grandfather's land? And how would his fingerprints get on the meth production materials? He'd insisted they not touch any of it. Too much still didn't make sense.

Likewise, she doubted her story made sense to the sheriff. He looked unconvinced when she told him about the plane shooting them out of the sky. Granted, it wasn't likely the kind of situation the small-town Iowa sheriff was used to encountering, but she didn't appreciate the wary-eyed look he gave her.

Almost as though he didn't believe her.

He didn't think she was making drugs with Cutch, did he?

If Gideon Bromley suspected her of anything, he didn't mention it but simply clarified a few points in her report before he doffed his hat, hopped behind the wheel of the cruiser and drove away.

Elise spun around and faced her uncle, who'd been mostly silent through the whole exchange.

"I didn't know they were going to do that," he said simply. "They asked if Cutch was with you. I didn't think—"

"It's okay." Elise pinched her face up. She wouldn't cry, though the morning had already been overwhelming and it wasn't even near lunchtime yet. "Do you think he's guilty?"

Leroy shrugged. "Sounds like they've got a pretty solid case."

Elise could guess what her uncle was thinking: "And he's a McCutcheon."

Her uncle didn't respond to her comment. His eyes followed the dust cloud that trailed behind the sheriff's car. "Come on." He headed back toward the plane. "You want to fly or you want me to?"

Feeling guilty about the crashed crop duster that was still lying sideways in a ditch on the next road south, Elise asked, "Where are we headed?"

"Back to the airfield. I have to prep the next load for Rodney."

"Oh? Did he finally show up for work?"

"Yeah. Turns out he overslept." Leroy stopped by the door of the plane and looked at her questioningly.

"You can fly," Elise told him, glad she didn't have to do it. After everything she'd been through, not even flying appealed to her anymore.

Fortunately, the short flight was uneventful. They landed at the airport before Elise realized she didn't have a vehicle. Cutch had given her a lift from his place. Her car was still at home. She wondered if he would mind if she drove his truck. But then again she didn't have his keys.

Leroy did the postflight check on her plane, and Elise walked in a daze toward the parking lot. She paused, her numb mind slugging through the unappealing choices before her. The phone in her pocket began to chirp.

"Hello?"

"Elise, I need your help," Cutch's words were hushed, almost as though he didn't want to be overheard.

"Where are you?" she asked, surprised that he'd be calling her. Wasn't he supposed to be in jail?

"In jail." He sighed. "This is what's called a booking call. I only get one."

And he'd chosen her? She almost felt flattered.

Cutch continued quickly, "Remember the red mud we saw on the bottom of the plane?"

"Yes."

"There's only one place in the county with red mud like that—Bruce Bromley's place. I was just out there this past spring for a reassessment. That's when I discovered all the improvements he's made—inground swimming pool, new outbuildings and an airstrip."

Elise sucked in her breath. "The sheriff's older brother! That's how the gunmen knew where to find us. He was getting his information straight from the top."

"I'm afraid so. Now listen. We can't trust the sheriff. They've got to be the ones who are framing me. I've got to get out of jail *today*. I heard the deputies talking. The judge is off for the Labor Day holiday, but when he comes back tomorrow, he'll probably raise my bail out of sight—we're talking millions. My only chance to get out and prove I'm innocent is if you bail me out today."

"I'd do it, Cutch, but I need ten thousand *cash* and collateral worth the other ninety thousand."

"You can put up my land as collateral," Cutch explained. "My wallet's in my truck. Let me give you my PIN. You'll have to withdraw the rest."

"Just a minute. I need something to write with."

While Elise let herself into the office to find a pen, Cutch's voice softened. "Are you hanging in there?"

She fumbled with the doorknob. "I'm pretty freaked out, I have to admit." She turned the knob and pushed the door open with her hip. "We *have* to catch these guys, Cutch. They're making drugs that will ruin people's lives just like they ruined your grandfather's life. We've got to bring them to justice. Okay, I've got a pen."

"Good girl." Cutch's smile carried through in his voice over the phone, and Elise's heart gave a little hitch as he told her the information she'd need to retrieve cash from his bank and credit lines at the ATM.

Did this determined man really trust her to bail him out? She felt hopeful that she'd be able to free him, but at the same time, doubts and fears tempered her optimism. She wasn't even sure he was innocent. Where had he gotten the money to buy his land, anyway? She imagined the sheriff could have faked the fingerprints—or even lied about it to save his brother's hide—but the land was a circumstantial complication she couldn't explain away.

"There's an extra key to the truck in the toolbox in back—passenger's side, in a magnetic keyholder up under the lid." Cutch's voice faltered. "Thank you so much for doing this, Elise."

"No problem," she stated simply. "I've got to get going." They said their goodbyes, and after another thank-you from Cutch, Elise shoved her phone back in her pocket and took a deep breath, approaching the more-or-less unfamiliar truck with her shoulders thrown back and her head held high. She tried to think courageous thoughts, because she certainly didn't feel courageous.

The key wasn't difficult to find. The truck started on the first try, and although Elise instinctively pulled on the lever by the steering wheel, thus dousing the windshield with wiper fluid and streaking dead bug residue across its previously mostly clean surface, she quickly found the gearshift on the floor and got the truck moving.

"Okay, Lord, I just need a little help," she prayed as she brought the full-size pickup around in a wide turn. She thought she had enough room to maneuver in the gravel lot, but she swiped close by the marigolds planted along one edge and, looking back, realized she'd flattened most of them. "Actually, Lord, I need a lot of help."

* * *

She made it back to her dad's farm without further incident. Her plan was to leave the truck there and take her car into town. Plus, she needed to grab her purse, because she knew the banks would be closed for Labor Day, and she doubted Cutch's cards would yield the full ten thousand at the ATM. She'd probably have to use some of her own money for the rest.

Her father was in the yard raking the first of autumn's leaves when she pulled in. He watched as she pulled Cutch's truck to a stop with wide berth between the front bumper and their white picket fence. No sense getting too close.

"Young Cutch with you?" Bill McAlister asked.

"No." Elise figured he'd probably hear the story from Leroy soon enough, so she explained as she darted to the house. "He's in jail. I have to go bail him out." She paused at the screen door, unsure what else to say, then darted inside and bounded up the stairs two-at-a-time. She wasn't sure what had prompted her to confess what was going on, but she figured her father had a right to know. Anyway, she didn't have time to worry about that now.

Though she'd have loved to take time for a shower, there wasn't any time to spare. Cutch was right. If she didn't get him bailed out that afternoon, the Bromleys would see that he never got out of jail. Then they'd keep pouring out drugs and destroying innocent lives. She couldn't let that happen. She'd have to hurry.

Elise grabbed her purse from where it sat next to her Bible on top of her bureau. In her haste, she knocked the Bible to the floor, and it spilled open to the page where she'd left the bulletin from church. As she bent to pick it up, her eyes fell on the words Pastor Carmichael had preached on the day before. The words spoke straight to her harried heart, and she felt the frantic pace her of her heartbeat steady somewhat as she read from chapter six of Luke.

Love your enemies, do good to those who hate you, bless those who curse you, pray for those who mistreat you…do to others as you would have them do to you.

The words stopped her in her tracks, and she stared for a long moment at the open Bible before gently closing it and placing it back on her bureau. For as long as she could remember, McCutcheons and McAlisters had been enemies.

But if what the Bible said was true, she was supposed to love them, do good to them, bless them, even pray for them, regardless of how they felt about her. Recalling what Pastor Carmichael had said in his sermon on the subject, Elise was reminded that God loved all His children, whether they loved Him back or not. And God called all His children to love their brothers and sisters with the same kind of love: a love that didn't demand to be loved in return.

So what difference did it make if Cutch had betrayed her all those years ago? That was his problem, not hers. The only reason she'd felt humiliated was because she'd truly loved him, and he obviously hadn't loved her back.

Love your enemies. The thought seemed to awaken a long-dormant part of her, as though the light had suddenly been switched on after she'd spent too long sleeping in the darkness. It didn't matter if Cutch loved her or not. It didn't matter if he hated her. God instructed her to love him.

There was no shame in loving Cutch. Even if he never returned her feelings, love didn't have to be returned to be real. She could love him today and eight years ago and for the rest of her life, and whether he loved her back or not, at least she knew she was doing God's will.

Love your enemies. Do good to those who hate you. Pray for them.

Taking the words to heart, Elise made her way slowly down the stairs, praying aloud as she went, "Lord, please be with Cutch while he's in jail. Help me to help him get out of there. And if I'm supposed to love him, Lord, then give me the strength to forgive him." As she stepped toward the front door, Elise's heart felt a little lighter. Cutch had said he wanted to be friends. Though she doubted they could ever be close buddies, maybe, with God's help, they could somehow move beyond the feud that afflicted their families. Elise opened the door, stepped outside into the bright sunlight and blinked.

Her father was waiting for her. "Now, what's this about Cutch being in jail?" he asked. "I've told you for years McCutcheons are nothing but trouble. And now you're planning to bail him out?"

Planting her feet solidly against the worn floorboards of the front porch, Elise looked up at her father, returning his gaze directly. He was right. He'd always insisted Cutch was trouble, and, except for those couple of months when they'd dated, she'd always believed her father was right. Now she wasn't so sure.

Granted, Cutch had publicly rejected and embarrassed her eight years before, but hadn't he indicated that morning that there was more to the story than she knew? Maybe it was time to follow her heart and trust Cutch for once.

"Yes, Dad. I'm going to bail him out, if I can. He's not as awful a person as you say he is." As she spoke the words, Elise realized just how true they were. Cutch had gone out of his way to help her, putting her needs before his own. He might not have ended up in jail if he'd chosen

to look for the anhydrous tank first instead of helping her
with her glider, but because she'd been so distraught, he'd
helped her.

Just because Cutch hadn't really loved her eight years
before didn't make him a bad person. She recalled his
plea that they be friends. Was it possible? She could start
finding out by springing him out of jail.

"I need to go, Dad. Cutch needs my help," Elise
explained before she turned and hurried to her car. She
didn't look back.

The ATM at the First Bank of Holyoake held a surprising amount of money, Elise discovered. Though their
bank cards were limited to withdrawals of two hundred
dollars per day, she was able to pull out a thousand dollars
on her credit card and thirty-five hundred with Cutch's
card, though she hated to think what the accompanying
fees might be.

But fees were nothing considering the alternative.
Between the cash she'd already withdrawn to take with
her on her scrapped trip to the Labor Day Powered Glider
Festival and the cash she'd found in Cutch's wallet, she
came up with a total of almost six thousand dollars.

So she was still over four thousand dollars short.

Elise drove around town and tried using their cards at
other ATMs, only to receive the message that she'd already
maxed out her withdrawals for the day. Although she'd
known that much already, she couldn't think of any other
option. Unsure where she might come up with another
four thousand dollars in cash, she followed her rumbling
stomach back home. It was past lunchtime.

Her father was just bringing meat in from the grill—
not charred burgers this time but steaks. She followed

him inside and watched as he pulled a couple of baked potatoes from the microwave.

"Hungry?" he asked.

"Starving," she admitted, plunking down her cash-filled purse with a sigh. Looking at the juicy steaks, she asked, "What's the occasion?"

"I think it's time you and I had a talk."

Dread filled her. Maybe she should have kept the whole bailing-Cutch-out-of-jail plan under wraps—at least until she knew if she'd be successful or not. And maybe she shouldn't have challenged her father so directly. She silently helped her father by setting the table while he pulled butter and sour cream from the fridge.

"Let's bless it," he said and bowed his head.

Elise obediently followed suit. She tried to focus on her father's prayer while impatience and despair waged war inside her. She needed to do *something* to come up with another four thousand dollars, not just sit there enjoying a steak lunch. But as her father's prayer tugged at her consciousness like lift pulling up on an airplane's wing, she realized he was praying for more than just their meal. Her father prayed for forgiveness—from God and from her.

Bill McAlister said, "Amen." Then he proceeded to cut into his steak. "Well done," he assessed with a satisfied nod. "How's yours?"

Somewhere midprayer, the churning in Elise's stomach had been replaced with an out-of-place peaceful feeling that she couldn't justify. As requested, she cut into her steak. "Medium rare," she informed him.

"That left burner's going out," her father grumbled. "Want me to put it back on?"

"No, really, it's fine. I don't like it charred." She wished he'd get on with whatever it was he was going to talk about.

Popping a bite in her mouth, she chewed slowly in hopes
he wouldn't expect her to talk as long as she had food in
her mouth.

As though he'd picked up on her impatience, Bill McAlister cleared his throat. "Did anyone ever tell you why
the McCutcheons and the McAlisters hate each other so
much?"

Elise blinked and continued chewing, "I know the feud
goes back a long time," she said once she'd swallowed her
bite of meat. "Didn't the McCutcheons sabotage grandpa's crop duster? But they were already rivals long before
that."

"Well, yes and no," her father qualified. "It's true that
eighty years ago, the McCutcheons and McAlisters ran
rival airstrips. After World War II, when crop dusting was
the new thing, there was a lot of competition between the
two families, but I don't think you'd ever say we hated one
another.

"To tell the truth, I felt sorry for the McCutcheons. They
say Old Cutch's dad was never the same after he came back
from the war. I was too young to know the difference,
but I do recall that he was a bum for years before he died
when Cutch was a young teenager. He left their family at
a terrible disadvantage. The man just didn't seem to have
his head on straight."

Elise nodded as her father recounted what had happened so many years before. His version of the story fit
with what Cutch had told her about his grandfather being
addicted to meth, but it didn't explain how the feud got
started. The families sounded like friendly rivals—a far
cry from the hatred that ran between them for her whole
life.

Bill continued with his story. "When your grandfather's
crop duster crashed and killed him, the McCutcheons were

the first to offer to help. Now, I suppose it was just human nature when some people jumped to the conclusion that the McCutcheons had something to do with your grandfather's plane going down, what with our two families being rivals and all. But your grandpa had a bad cold that day. He shouldn't have been flying, but you don't tell a stubborn man like that what to do. He took a bunch of cold medicine and went out. I imagine…" Her father's voice faded, full of emotion.

Elise didn't need her father to finish. She knew how alert a pilot needed to be to successfully maneuver the often-narrow confines above a field. A single error could bring a plane down.

Bill McAlister swallowed another bite of steak before continuing.

"Uncle Leroy was in the Air Force, and I'd been planning to join up, too, but after your grandpa died, I didn't see how I could do it. Old Cutch, he offered to watch over the business while we were gone. I thought Old Cutch was a good enough man, and he was one of the few people around who knew anything about flying, so I entrusted him with everything when I left."

Her dad stopped and sawed into his steak, and Elise watched him eat with a growing sense of foreboding. If her father had trusted the McCutcheons so much and didn't blame them for the accident that had killed her grandfather, then what had happened to cause him to turn against them so completely?

Bill McAlister took a long drink of his tea before continuing. His voice sounded a little uneven when he began again.

"When I went off to war, I left a ring on the finger of Anita Scarth. We were engaged to be married. She said she'd wait for me." His mouth twitched, and he worked his face into a grimace. He looked down and fiddled with a napkin, clearing his throat before continuing on.

"When I came home two years later, thinking I was going to get married, Anita was already a McCutcheon. Even in her letters, she never let on. But there she was, married a full year and pregnant with Young Cutch." His strong hands flexed emptily. "I've never spoken a kind word to a McCutcheon since. That's when I stopped denying those rumors about the McCutcheons sabotaging your grandpa's plane. That's when the feud really began."

Bill McAlister turned his attention back to his lunch, and Elise tried to process everything her dad had confessed. He'd loved Anita long ago? But Cutch was less than two years older than she was, and if her father had come home expecting to marry Anita, how had her father fallen in love with her mother so quickly?

She asked her father about the one point she couldn't work past. "How does my mother fit into all of this?"

Bill McAlister's eyes dropped, and he looked shamefully at his hands. "I was angry. I felt betrayed. I ran off to Missouri and got a job, figured I'd make Anita jealous or something. I met this pretty girl, and she was mad at her boyfriend, too. We thought we had so much in common with all our anger and feeling jilted that we couldn't see we were all wrong for each other. Sometimes I don't think your mother ever really loved me. And I suppose, truth be told, I didn't love her the way she deserved to be loved, either."

Elise could barely speak. "Is that—" she took a leveling breath, her lunch forgotten "—the guy she was mad at?"

Bill nodded. "He's her husband now. They patched things up when you were about a year old. They wanted to start a new life together. She tried to take you, too. She begged me to let you go. But Elise—" her father looked her in the eyes for the first time the whole meal "—you were all I had left. You were my little copilot. You were a true McAlister who loved planes and flying. 'Plane' was the second word you learned to say, right after 'Da-da.' I couldn't let her take you. We tried to make things work on your account, but finally she agreed to let you stay with me as long as I'd grant her a divorce."

While Elise struggled to come to grips with what her father had revealed, he pushed his plate back with a sigh.

"So that's it, then." Bill McAlister sighed. "I thought I could spare you from ever experiencing what I went through. I thought if I could just keep you away from Cutch, you'd be okay." He shook his head, regret simmering in the unshed tears in his eyes. "I've done wrong by maligning Cutch all these years. But how can I begin to make it up to you?"

For a few long minutes, Elise sat in stunned silence, at a loss for what to tell her father. All that hatred between their families all those years, and look where it had gotten them. Cutch was in jail, and she might be there soon if she wasn't careful. Something sparked in the back of her mind, and she snapped her head up.

"How much cash do you have?" she asked breathlessly.

"How much do you need?"

"Over four thousand dollars."

Her father gave a low whistle. "I don't have that kind of cash on hand, but we could go to the bank."

"They're closed for Labor Day," Elise reminded him.

"Well—" Bill McAlister took their empty plates and carried them to the sink "—then we'll see what we can do."

Elise explained as much as she could to her father on

the way to the ATM, including their suspicions about the Bromleys and the involvement of Donnie and Darrel. From the disparaging looks her father gave her, she could tell he wasn't pleased about the whole getting-shot-out-of-the-sky-twice thing. But he withdrew as much cash as he could and handed it over, apologizing that he hadn't been able to withdraw more than three thousand dollars.

"Don't apologize, Dad. You've done a lot," Elise thanked him. "I just don't know where we're going to come up with another thousand bucks."

"You know what I think?" her father asked as she finished stuffing the cash into her wallet and pulled away from the ATM. "I think if it's the McCutcheon's son in jail, they should contribute to the fund that bails him out."

Elise stopped at the outlet of the parking lot and stared at her father. "You want us to go to the McCutcheons for money?" she asked incredulously. If Cutch had only had one booking call, it was likely his parents didn't even know he was in jail.

Her father mulled the question until a horn beeped impatiently behind them. Elise pulled forward, heading out of town in the direction of the McCutcheon farm.

"I think," her father said slowly, "it's time we all talk."

"Okay," Elise agreed shakily, hardly able to believe that for the second time in one day—and for the second time in her life—she was about to visit the McCutcheon farm. Only this time it was to tell them their son was in jail and to ask them for a thousand dollars to free him.

She didn't envision that conversation going well.

TWELVE

"Did you want to wait in the car?" Elise offered as she pulled to a stop where Cutch's truck had been parked that morning.

"I'm not afraid." Bill McAlister's words were betrayed by the slight tremble in his voice.

Elise didn't blame him. This was almost as bad as getting shot out of the sky—in some ways worse. She rang the front bell and was relieved when Anita answered the door; since no one in town was aware of Old Cutch's condition, Elise feared her father would be shocked to see him. As long as he stayed out of sight, she figured they could get through their visit, although she immediately caught the look that passed between her father and Cutch's mom. Those two had been engaged once, years ago. Now Anita McCutcheon eyed Bill McAlister warily.

"Can I help you?"

Knowing Cutch had used his lone call to phone her, Elise realized Anita probably had no idea what kind of trouble Cutch was in. "I'm sorry to bother you, but Cutch is in trouble," Elise began.

A worried look crossed Anita's face. "Does this have anything to do with the law?" she asked. "Sheriff Bromley came by looking for him just after you two left this morning."

"That's just it," Elise started but quickly choked up on the words.

Her father patted her back. "Young Cutch is in jail," he explained. "We need a little more than a thousand dollars in cash to bail him out."

"Oh." Anita looked stunned but opened the door wider for them to pass through. "Come in. I—I guess I'll need to talk to my husband."

As she led them through to the parlor, Elise's father caught her eye. "It'll be okay," he mouthed to her.

Elise offered him back a weak smile. As far as coming up with the money went, she knew her father was probably right. Even if they didn't have the cash on hand, she didn't doubt the McCutcheons would come up with the rest of what they needed to free their son.

No, bailing Cutch out of jail no longer worried her so much. She just wasn't sure how she could keep her feelings a secret now that she'd realized she didn't hate him after all.

Elise drove as fast as the law would allow and arrived at the jail after having dropped her father off at home on her way back to town. She hurried inside the building hauling a purse full of cash. Ten thousand dollars right on the nose. She and Anita had counted it twice with trembling hands.

The release process took just over a half hour. At first Elise felt surprised that Sheriff Bromley let Cutch go so easily. Then she felt suspicious.

When she and Cutch were finally alone together in her car and he'd thanked her for what must have been the twentieth time and promised to pay back every penny he owed her plus interest, instead of saying, "You're welcome," she put the car in reverse and said, "They're up to something. I don't have a good feeling about this. Do you think we should get out of town?"

"Jump bail?" Cutch shook his head. "I'd lose my farm and get in a whole lot of trouble."

"You're in a whole lot of trouble now." Elise steered the car more or less on autopilot and found herself headed toward home. "Unless you can prove what the Bromleys are up to."

"If we could find where they'd moved their production operation, then we'd have something. My guess is Bruce wasn't expecting to have to move it until you flew over and messed up his plans. He may not have had an alternate location."

"Maybe he took it to his place. We could head out there and see if we could spot anything."

"And get shot at again? I was just out assessing his property a few months ago. He's got an eight-foot privacy fence all around his farm. The place is locked up like a fort, and I can't tell you how many Doberman pinschers he has guarding it. They didn't look friendly, either."

"Then what can we do?" Elise felt desperate.

"We need to get in touch with the federal authorities," Cutch reasoned aloud, "but we need something more for them to look at than some ruts in the ground. Right now it's my word against the Bromleys, and you can guess who everybody's going to believe. You're the only person who thinks I'm innocent."

"And your parents," Elise corrected him but still felt her conscience twist at his statement. True, she mostly believed he was innocent. There was no way she would have put up her own money to bail him out if she hadn't believed that. And she'd asked God to help her trust him, though there was still one question that irked her. She cleared her throat, "Say Cutch?"

"Yes?"

"Where'd you get the money?" Though her words had come out of nowhere and she wasn't able to muster a very clear question, Cutch seemed to understand what she was getting at.

"To buy Grandpa's land?"

She nodded and kept her eyes glued to the road, though she'd driven the route thousands of times and the most dangerous hazard she had to watch for were the pesky grasshoppers that crunched under her tires as she drove.

"I saved up my money—"

Elise interrupted him. "Hundreds of thousands of dollars?"

"For part of it," Cutch added quickly. "But a lot of the money came from my little sister, Ginny. She wanted me to put it in something where she'd earn a return, and land is a good investment."

"Where did Ginny get that kind of cash?" Elise found it hard to believe a woman younger than she was could amass that kind of fortune. Ginny had been gone for years, out East somewhere, though Elise didn't listen to gossip about Cutch's little sister any more than she listened to gossip about his father's health. Now she wished she'd paid more attention.

"I'm not supposed to tell anyone, but I'm tired of keeping secrets. She's an aviatrix out East—she's made a lot of money in her barnstorming flight shows."

Elise turned past the windbreak into the driveway of the McAlister farm. Though she was amazed at Ginny's colorful occupation, as the farm fell into view, she saw a sight that distracted her from her questions.

Her father and Uncle Leroy were waiting for them,

sitting in the rocking chairs on the front porch with their shotguns on their laps.

"Uh, maybe I shouldn't be here," Cutch's strong voice wavered.

But Elise's conversation with her father was still fresh on her mind, and she couldn't believe her dad would change his mind about Cutch again. "Just a second," she whispered to Cutch, parking the car and hopping out. She called out to her father, "What's up with the guns, Dad?"

Her father looked down at his weapon while Uncle Leroy answered aggressively, "We're hunting Bromleys."

Elise ducked her head back into the car. "It's okay," she assured Cutch. "They're on our side."

Though he looked less-than-certain, Cutch climbed out of the car and hurried after her up the path to the porch.

As they approached, Elise's father explained, "I went to the airfield to tell Leroy what you'd said, including the part about Donnie Clark and Darrel Stillwater working for Bruce Bromley."

Uncle Leroy cut in. "Rodney was in the office while your dad explained things to me. He knows where they took that tank. See, he about ran into Donnie and Darrel on his way home Saturday. They were pulling onto the highway in a red truck pulling an anhydrous ammonia tank."

Elise gasped. The men could have moved the tank right after they'd slashed Cutch's tires. With a half mile of tree-filled hills between them, Cutch and Elise would have never heard them.

Cutch filled in, "My land is up by Rodney's place."

"Isn't that your grandpa's old pecan grove?" Bill McAlister clarified.

For a moment, Cutch faltered, as though reluctant to

admit he owned the failed property. But his hesitation lasted only a couple of seconds. "Yes. That's where Elise's glider went down on Saturday. It's where we first spotted the tank."

"That sounds like the spot," Leroy confirmed, as Rodney stepped out of the house with a can of cola. "You tell the rest," Leroy prompted Rodney.

"About following Donnie and Darrel?" Rodney clarified. When everyone nodded, the older man jumped into the story. "I was bored anyway and itching for something to do. When I saw those two try to pull out right in front of me hauling that tank, I knew they must be in an awful hurry for something. And anyway, everybody knows Donnie Clark's a meth addict. He's jumpy all the time, and his teeth are gone. You don't have to know much to know a meth addict pulling a tank of anhydrous ain't a good combination, especially when Donnie doesn't do any farming. So I waited for them to get a couple hills in front of me, then I followed them." Rodney took a long drink of his cola.

"Where did they end up?" Cutch asked.

"Bruce Bromley's place. They were let in through that big gateway he's got there. I just drove on past like I was headed someplace else. Thought about maybe calling the sheriff, but then, what did I know? Two guys moved a tank? Nothing illegal about that." Rodney finished with his characteristic nervous laugh.

Elise looked back and forth between her father and her uncle, who were both gripping their guns awfully tightly. "So now what? You two want to head down there for some vigilante justice?"

"What else can we do?" Leroy asked gruffly. "Bruce Bromley is the sheriff's brother. If the law is in on the wrong side, we have to take matters into our own hands."

Cutch shook his head. "The sheriff still has to answer to somebody. We need to get in touch with the DEA—the Drug Enforcement Agency. I learned a thing or two about them a few years back." He looked at Elise sheepishly, and she smiled, deducing that he referred to that better-forgotten time when he'd been investigated for the research he'd done on meth.

Leroy didn't look like he wanted to let go of his gun, but Bill McAlister eased himself up from his rocking chair. "I suppose I could look them up and give them a call," he said, heading for the front door.

"Go ahead." His brother stood and headed after him. "But if they give you the rub-off, we'll do this ourselves!"

As Rodney followed the brothers inside, Cutch turned to Elise. "Do you think they'll be okay if we steal a moment alone?"

The intense look in his eyes made Elise's heart flutter like a Dacron wing on a windy day. "Where do you want to go?" she asked, trying to ignore the thrill she felt as he took her hand and tugged her off the porch.

"Some place a little more private than this," he said, leading her toward the barn.

Elise tried to calm her heart as she followed him. She was a grown woman, and she'd long ago grown out of her delusional hopes that Cutch might someday return her affection.

Cutch pulled her behind the barn and started speaking without preamble. "My father's had cancer for eight years, Elise," he started. "When he was first diagnosed, he insisted that he would kick the disease without anyone ever knowing he was sick. This was less than a year after

he'd finally been appointed president of the bank—his
lifelong dream. He was afraid if anyone knew he was sick
that they'd think he couldn't do his job."

Though the length of elapsed time struck her as vaguely
significant, Elise couldn't figure out why Cutch would
want to discuss his father's health when so many far more
important issues were looming. But she kept her mouth
shut and let him continue.

"At the same time, he knew it was important to reduce
the stress factors in his life in order for his treatment to be
successful." Cutch still held Elise's hand and now looked
down, squeezing her fingers gently. "Our relationship was
a source of anguish for him." Cutch pinched his eyes shut
and swallowed.

Elise's mind raced ahead. "Did he ask you to break up
with me?"

"No," Cutch denied. "His only request was that I not
tell anyone about his condition. Nobody could know. Especially not you." His blue eyes bore into hers. "I found out
my father had cancer the day before Sam and Phoebe's
wedding. I was afraid that if I stood up in front of all our
relatives and friends and announced that I was in love with
my father's enemy's daughter that it would kill him."

The anguish of Cutch's decision tore through Elise. "So
you thought you had to choose…"

"I had to choose between my father's life and your
love. Believe me, Elise, I wrestled with that decision—
probably more than I should have." He hung his head as
though ashamed. "We were so young. I still had a year
left of college. You were only nineteen. We'd been dating
for, what, ten weeks? How could I do that to my father—"
Cutch's throat made a strangled sound "—when he didn't
have long to live?"

"Why didn't you tell me?" Elise struggled to understand.

"I know he didn't want you to talk about his cancer, but couldn't you have at least given me some explanation?"

"I tried. I wanted to talk to you before the wedding, but you were too busy with all the wedding things. Then, afterward, I pulled you behind the curtains on the stage thinking I'd finally get a moment alone with you. I was just going to explain what I could and leave out the part about my dad's health, but you looked so beautiful." Cutch leaned against the solid wood of the barn and pulled her close to him. He reached out a tentative hand and tucked a stray lock of hair behind her ear.

Just as he had that night. Elise felt her lips tingling at the memory of the kiss they'd shared. She'd dreamed of that moment for weeks, only to have it pulled away from her so quickly.

"I promise you, Elise, I had no idea my cousins were going to pull the curtain open. They caught us at the worst possible moment."

Whatever tenderness she'd felt at the memory of the kiss they'd shared was shattered as she recalled what had happened next. "You laughed at me," she reminded Cutch, pulling back from where he stood so close to her.

"I will regret that until the day I die. Everybody else was laughing, and I didn't know how else to respond. I was young and stupid, and my father was sitting right there at the front table, watching us. I didn't think. I'm so sorry."

Elise inhaled a shaky breath, still unsure how she felt about Cutch's explanation. Too much had hit her too quickly. And they still had to catch the Bromleys.

"Where are you? Elise?" Bill McAlister's voice echoed through the farmyard. Immediately wondering if he'd been able to contact the authorities, she straightened and took a step away from Cutch.

"We should find out what's happening."

Out on a Limb

"You're right." Cutch agreed with a nod, though he looked a little disappointed.

Elise felt a similar twinge. Their relationship had never had a shot at getting off the ground eight years before. And it seemed forces were conspiring to keep them apart again.

She trotted around the side of the barn. "Yeah, Dad?"

"You've got visitors." Her father explained simply.

A gleaming white motor home and matching trailer sat parked in front of her father's house. Elise recognized the custom mural of gliders in flight that decorated the sides.

"Vera! Bob!" she exclaimed, running to greet her friends from the paraglider festival she'd missed. "What are you doing here?"

"Oh, good, you *are* here." A smartly dressed older woman hopped out of the motor home and headed for Elise.

Elise hugged the spiky-haired woman and the balding man who was with her, glad that she'd gotten a chance to see her friends after all, though their timing felt awkward.

The older woman explained. "We couldn't very well pass so close to your farm and not stop to say hello, especially after that distressing e-mail you sent. I want to see this glider of yours that was shot down. I told Bob I just can't believe it until I see it with my own eyes."

Cutch hung back to talk to Bill while Elise and her friends went to the barn and looked at Elise's glider.

"Were you able to contact the DEA?"

Bill McAlister shrugged. "They took down all the information I could give them and said they'd set up surveillance on Bruce Bromley's place to determine if there was anything behind my tip. They hoped to know something in a matter of weeks."

Cutch shook his head. "We need help *now*."

"I know. But don't mention that to Leroy. He's liable to go shoot somebody."

From what Cutch understood of Leroy McAlister, he'd spent a couple of decades in the Air Force before returning to Holyoake to run the family crop dusting business. He was the type who liked to go in guns blazing. While that might be great in battle, it wouldn't be a good idea in Holyoake County. "We've got him all riled up about this," Cutch said, realizing this regretfully.

"I'll see if I can't get him calmed down. We'll head out to the airstrip. That ought to distract him." Bill looked off in the direction Elise had disappeared. "You keep an eye on Elise for now."

"Sounds good." With a nod to Bill, Cutch headed off after Elise, his heart warmed by the fact Bill had entrusted him with his daughter. Did Elise's father trust him now? It would change his world if he did.

At the same time, Cutch felt impatient. If something wasn't done soon, Bruce and Gideon would no doubt move their drug lab again, this time to someplace no one would find it. To cover their trail, they'd likely come up with reasons for throwing him right back in jail. He doubted he'd get out so easily this time. He ducked into the barn and listened with half an ear as Elise chatted with Vera and Bob.

From what he could tell from their conversation, Vera and Bob were power gliding enthusiasts who'd attended the festival in Kansas City that Elise had been so disappointed to miss. The older pair raved about the new set of gliders they'd bought from a dealer at the festival. As Bob explained their need to sell off their older pair of gliders, a light went off in Cutch's mind.

"Do you have them with you?" he asked, cutting off Bob in the middle of his long-winded explanation about the features that might boost the older gliders' selling price.

"The gliders? Of course. We weren't sure we'd be buying new ones, so we had them with us to fly. They're in the trailer."

"Can we take a look at them?" Cutch read the man's startled features and added, "Elise needs a new glider, you know. And I've always been interested in the sport. If we pick up a used pair for a decent price—"

"Oh, yes. Right this way!" Bob's face brightened at Cutch's suggestion, and he led them back in the way of the trailer.

Elise gave Cutch a confused look and whispered, "You've always been interested in the sport?"

"Sure. Don't you remember when I attended your tutorial at the county fair? I thought I took to it pretty well."

"True." Elise still sounded hesitant.

Bob pulled open the rear door of the trailer and hauled out a heavy bag that held a folded glider. As the older man pulled out the glider and began setting it up for inspection, Cutch peppered him with questions on how to operate the machine, and finally, satisfied the gear would meet his needs, he got down to asking Bob what he'd want for both gliders.

No sooner had they settled on a price than Elise pulled on his shirtsleeve. "Could you excuse us just a moment?" she asked her friends with a polite smile. But when she cornered Cutch over by his truck, her smile was gone.

"What do you think you're doing?" she asked, a slight screech underscoring her words.

"Don't you think they're nice gliders? Or is the price too high?"

Elise set her hands on her hips and glared at him. "Of course they're gorgeous gilders. Bob and Vera only buy the best. But what do you need a glider for all of a sudden?"

Cutch smiled, convinced his plan was a good one. Bruce Bromley's place was locked up tight on all sides—no doubt the man felt confident he could securely hide his operation there, if only temporarily. That left them with only one possible means of access to the evidence he guarded behind those eight-foot walls. "We'll use the gliders to fly over Bruce Bromley's place. We can take pictures—"

"And get shot out of the sky again?" Elise shook her head angrily. "I don't think so."

"We'll be stealthy. In and out."

"It won't work anyway, Cutch. You can't take pictures and fly a glider at the same time. You have to hold on to the speed bar to control the glider. The minute you try to take a picture, you lose control of your glider. Trust me. I've tried a dozen different ways of doing it. I've mounted the camera to my glider. I've mounted it to my helmet, to my windsuit and even to my gloves. It doesn't matter where you put it. The second you try to operate the camera, you're a danger to yourself and a menace to anyone on the ground below you."

"What if you didn't have to operate the camera?"

Elise's face crinkled up and she shoved her hair back behind her ears. "I don't see how that would—"

"Can you just trust me?" Cutch realized he was running out of time and didn't feel he could spare the time it would take to explain every little detail of his plans. Besides, he wasn't exactly sure how he was going to rig the cameras. But he felt certain he could make his plan work. He'd have to.

"Trust you?" Elise's warm eyes simmered with uncertainty. "Cutch, I bailed you out of jail. I put up my own money in addition to yours. I'm trying to help you catch these drugmakers, but Cutch—" the hitch in her voice stilled her volume to almost nothing "—I'm going out on a limb here as it is."

Cutch reached for her and let his hands fall gently on her shoulders. She flinched at first but didn't pull away. "I appreciate that. You've taken on enormous challenges, and I feel awful for what you've had to go through—"

"It's not just that." Elise wriggled out from under his hands. "I learned some things from my dad today about the feud and about my mother. And then all that stuff you just told me about your dad...I still haven't decided how I feel about everything."

The enormity of everything Elise was dealing with settled in the air around them. As much as he wanted to wrap his arms around her and try to comfort her, Cutch realized Elise needed her space. He'd been thrust back into her life two days before, and though in his heart he wanted to mend their friendship and make her a part of his life again, he realized she probably wasn't ready to do that yet. She might never be. "Do you want me to just get out of here?" he asked quietly.

Elise looked up at him with wide eyes. "I don't know how that would do any good if the Bromley brothers are after us." She looked over to where Bob had pulled the second glider from the trailer and was busy setting it up for their inspection. Cutch could see indecision warring in her features. "Maybe you're right. Maybe we need to be proactive, to go after them instead of waiting for them to catch us."

"I don't want to put you in danger," Cutch qualified.

With a shrug, Elise acknowledged, "I'm already in

danger. I just—" she shook off her defeated posture and raised her shoulders, tilting her chin up in a brave face he could tell drew on what little reserves of courage she had left "—I'm going to trust. I'm going to trust God and trust you."

"Thank you." He started to reach for her, wanting to tuck the loose hair behind her ears for her again, to reach out and feel the softness of her cheek and her silky smooth hair, but he recalled the way she'd wriggled away from him only moments before. He might want to be friends again, but obviously she wasn't ready to return his feelings yet. The last thing he wanted to do was push her away. "First things first. I need to figure out if I can fly one of these contraptions."

"And then?" Elise met his eyes.

"Then, if we can, we're going to find some real evidence to lock these guys away."

THIRTEEN

They spent the next half hour in flying drills. Fortunately, Cutch remembered everything he'd learned at her glider tutorial, which gave them a solid foundation to build on. When Elise was satisfied that Cutch had the basics down, she allowed him to write a check to Vera and Bob for the gliders; then she hugged them and waved as they headed off on their way. Though they'd used all their cash for bail money, Cutch still had money in the bank to cover the check.

Fortunately, Cutch was a natural when it came to flying. After all, it ran in his family. Under any other circumstances, Elise would have wanted her pupil to practice over the course of several weeks before attempting a potentially dangerous flight, but she couldn't see any way around what they needed to do. They couldn't trust the sheriff—or anyone in the sheriff's office—as far as that went. And they had to assemble some sort of evidence against the Bromleys—soon. Elise had no doubt the brothers would be coming after them again. They'd let Cutch go far too easily, and the only explanation was that they planned to simply arrest him again, probably on stickier charges the next time.

"Now what?" Elise asked Cutch as her friends' motor home and trailer rumbled off down the road.

"Do you have any old cameras that still work that you don't mind me tinkering with?"

"Sure." As a photographer, Elise had a soft spot for cameras, and with the rate new technology developed, she'd amassed several that had been replaced by newer models with more impressive features, though the older cameras were still perfectly usable.

Cutch continued, "Do you have any electrical wire, wire strippers, tinning flux—"

"I don't even know what tinning flux is," Elise shook her head.

"Let me call Sam."

Cutch got on the phone with his cousin, who was an electrician. Elise recalled years before hearing about the projects the two of them had tinkered on together, even some county fair entries in their teenage years. They'd rigged some interesting gizmos, she remembered with clarity. It didn't take long for Cutch to explain to his cousin what he was up to.

"He'll bring what we need. Can you show me the cameras?"

They headed to the house, and Elise dug through a box in the closet where she stored her "spare" electronics. She sold a few of her older cameras from time to time, but since cameras were a photographer's eyes and hands, parting with them often felt like losing part of herself. So Elise had several for Cutch to choose from.

"We need something with a lot of memory and a big screen." He took one of the cameras she held out to him. "Does this have an easily accessible power switch?"

"Right on top." Elise reached over and showed him how to turn the camera on.

Nothing happened when he flipped the switch.

Cutch pushed the camera back toward her. "We're going to need a fully charged battery."

Pulling a cord from the camera's box, Elise said, "Just let me plug it in for a couple hours. It should charge right up."

She reached out to take the camera from him. Her fingers brushed his as he handed it over. She glanced up just long enough to meet his eyes and exchange a slight smile. Then she turned her attention back to the cameras and held up another for his inspection.

Working with Cutch felt natural, yet exhilarating. He was polite, capable and strong. Her heart gave a little twist, and she wondered how things might have been different if their relationship had gotten off the ground the first time around. Would they have lasted? Were they meant to? It was more than she could allow herself to be distracted by at the moment.

"I think these two will be best," Cutch announced with a satisfied sigh. He placed the rejected cameras back in the box and helped Elise lift the lot back into place on a shelf high in the closet before heading to the kitchen table to work.

While Elise stood back and observed, Cutch disassembled the battery and shutter parts of the two cameras he'd decided would best meet their needs. "We're going to rig these to take pictures automatically, one right after the other, from the moment we turn them on until the disk space runs out. I'm going to mount a camera on the speed bar of both gliders. We'll fly over Bruce Bromley's place, and once we spot something we can use as evidence, all we have to do is turn the camera on—one switch, one time. We'll barely have to let go of the speed bar. That won't throw us off too much, will it?"

Elise marveled at his invention. "One switch, one time? That shouldn't be a problem. I've been known to scratch my nose when I'm flying."

"Perfect," Cutch continued. "Then we just have to fly over long enough for the cameras to capture some decent shots. Once we have the evidence we need, we'll get out of there and call the Feds—hopefully before anyone sees us."

The plan sounded good to Elise, except for the last part about not being seen. But then, she figured she was still a little jumpy after being shot down a mere two days before. And anyway, she told herself, Bruce's goons would keep coming after her, whether she was flying in their airspace or her own. Heading straight toward their hideout might be the last thing they'd expect her to do—and therefore the last place they'd be looking for her.

Or so she tried to tell herself.

When Sam showed up, he and Cutch got to work on the cameras, and Elise stood back, watching them work. She couldn't help but smile as she watched Cutch bent in concentration over his project. He was always so devoted to whatever he was working on.

That had been one of the traits that had drawn her to him so strongly when they'd first met. She couldn't think of a guy who wouldn't have scoffed at the idea of cohosting a couple's wedding shower, but Cutch had thrown himself into the project and made the event memorable and exciting. She still remembered the photo slide show they'd labored endlessly over together and even the decorations Cutch had helped with.

He was a good guy. In her heart of hearts, she knew that, though she'd been so afraid for so long to accept that her feelings for him could possibly be real. He'd hurt her so much, just as her mother had hurt her by leaving.

But, if what her father had said was true, Elise realized her mother hadn't wanted to leave her after all. Her mother had actually loved her and tried to make a doomed marriage work just for her sake. The revelation turned everything she'd believed about her childhood right on its head and challenged all her previous assumptions about love.

She'd thought that love was a temperamental thing. Elusive, teasing, something to be desired but not trusted, something easily snatched away. Was it possible her mother loved her still? Her father's revelation made her wonder if it was possible. She wished he was around so she could ask him more about it, but he'd left with Leroy and Rodney while she was talking with Vera and Bob.

While she stood there feeling useless, Cutch and Sam kept up a lively conversation. "Do you know what Grandpa Scarth has been up to lately?" Cutch asked his cousin about their grandfather.

Sam chuckled. "So, you've noticed he's been up to something, too, have you? He keeps coming over to the house and having Phoebe help him on the computer. He's been ordering things online."

"What sorts of things?" Cutch asked, and Elise listened closely for the answer, knowing their grandfather drove a red truck that might fit the description of the one Cutch had spotted the day his tires were first slashed.

Sam shrugged, most of his attention focused on the electrical work on the cameras. "Don't know. He's awfully secretive about it, but he said something to Phoebe about a surprise. I didn't want to ask—thought it might have to do with Christmas presents or something."

Elise let out a frustrated sigh, and Cutch looked up from his project. He winked at her. "We're almost done. You're being patient. Thank you."

She shrugged off his thanks. "I feel a little useless right now."

"If you want, you can head out and make sure the gliders are ready to go. We're almost done here. Then all we have to do is duct tape the cameras into place and we can go."

"Okay," Elise said, certain her voice sounded far more confident than she felt. Cutch's plan still seemed a little risky to her, though she understood why they needed to locate the anhydrous ammonia tank and whatever other drugmaking paraphernalia Bruce would have moved from his operation on Cutch's land. If they waited any longer, Bruce Bromley would only have that much more time to move or destroy any evidence they might be able to find against him—or use it to pin the meth production on them. Elise wavered indecisively as she approached the gliders and looked them over to be sure they were ready for the upcoming flight.

A movement on the horizon caught her eye, and she looked out over the hills to where the vista gave way to a breathtaking view of rolling southwestern Iowa farmland. A white car topped the ridge of the highest hill between the McAlister farm and the McCutcheon place. For a second, Elise feared the sheriff was looking for Cutch again. Then she realized she'd seen that car before—parked in front of the McCutcheon place.

Elise hurried around to the front of the house just in time to see Anita McCutcheon pull to a stop in front of the white picket fence. She had her husband and father in the car with her. Never in her lifetime had the McCutcheons stepped foot on McAlister property. She wondered what could possibly have brought them her way.

Old Cutch rolled his window down. "Is my son around

here?" he asked with a glance toward where Cutch's indigo blue pickup sat where she'd parked it earlier.

"Yes. He's inside. He and Sam are working on a project." Elise wondered what had happened that had caused Old Cutch to leave his home—something big, obviously. "Do you want me to ask him to come outside?"

Opening the car door, Old Cutch lowered his feet to the ground, his bony white ankles showing between the cuffs of his slacks and the tops of his loafers. "That's all right. We'll all go in and talk like civilized people."

Elise nodded and hurried to hold the door for them. She called down the hall, "Cutch, your parents and grandfather are here."

"What?" Cutch jumped up and helped his father inside. "What's the occasion?" he asked.

"We need to talk," Old Cutch announced as he eased himself into a chair.

Sam looked uncomfortable. "I'll just get these cameras mounted," he offered and ducked out the back door.

Old Cutch nodded to Sam as he left, then gave Elise and Cutch each a long look in turn. "The sheriff came by the house earlier," he began.

A worried look crossed Cutch's face. "How long ago?"

"They left not ten minutes ago," Anita explained. "They were looking for you, Cutch. They had a warrant for your arrest with more charges this time. We sent them into town, then headed straight over here."

Elise looked over at Cutch and saw the same apprehension on his features as she was sure were evident on her own. Just as she'd feared, the sheriff hadn't wasted any time. If the sheriff caught up to him, he might never be able to clear his name.

Before Elise could decide how to respond, Sam came bursting back through the rear door of the house.

"I hate to interrupt, but I thought you needed to know that the sheriff's coming up the road."

"Are the cameras ready?" Elise asked as Cutch jumped to his feet.

Sam nodded. "They're mounted and ready to go."

Cutch looked from Sam to his parents and grandfather. "Stall the sheriff if you can. Then somebody needs to update Bill and Leroy on what's happening. They're at the airstrip. Tell them to call the DEA back and send them after Bruce and Gideon Bromley. They're guilty of producing meth, and we can prove it."

"You've got evidence against them?" Grandpa Scarth asked.

"No," Cutch admitted, "but we will by the time they get here."

Elise practically pushed Cutch out the back door while he was still talking. They ran for the gliders that were stashed behind the barn. Everything inside Elise shouted at her to hurry, to flee, to stay ahead of the sheriff before he could pin false charges on them both.

Cutch quickly checked the camera taped to the center of her speed bar before turning to inspect the camera taped to the other glider. She snapped her helmet into place and strapped herself hastily into the harness.

"Take off," he insisted as he donned his helmet.

"Are you sure you'll be okay?"

"I'm right behind you," he said, strapping himself into his glider's harness.

"Okay." Elise took a deep breath and ran down the field, fear fueling her. She could hear slamming doors echoing through the farmyard.

The sheriff and his men had arrived.

* * *

Cutch watched as Elise took lightly to the air. Then he ran down the field, silently reviewing in his mind the take-off procedure. It was fairly simple, really. All he had to do was start the engine and keep running until he was into the air.

Easy.

As long as he made it into the air before he came to the fence at the end of the field he'd be fine. During practice, with no pressure and Elise running alongside him cheering him on, it had seemed so simple.

Now his feet felt like lead and fear stole his breath as he charged down the field with the unfamiliar wings strapped above him. The soles of his running shoes pounded against the soft earth, and he kept waiting for the pull on his harness, for the weightless lift that would tell him he was doing it right.

He ought to feel it by now. "Dear Lord, help me out. *Please*," he began to pray.

Finally, the harness strapped around his torso seemed to grab hold of him and tug him into the air just as he drew near to the fence. He continued running as he took to the air, one foot touching the top rail of the fence and pushing off as the powered glider hoisted him into the sky.

Ahead of him, Elise seemed to be flying fairly low. He suspected she was hoping to avoid detection. Maybe if Sam and his folks made enough noise, the sheriff and his men wouldn't notice the sound like two lawn mowers taking off into the sky. Maybe they wouldn't see the streaks of white and teal tearing off toward the horizon.

Right. And maybe their crazy plan would work.

Cutch maneuvered his glider alongside Elise's and gestured with his head in the direction of Bruce Bromley's farm. "Let's get these pictures while the sheriff's distracted," he shouted.

Elise nodded, her face set in a determined expression that didn't hide the fear underneath. Cutch felt a wave of guilt that he'd let her get mixed up in all of this. He wished there was some other way to keep her safe from the Bromleys, but the only way to do that was to get the drug producers locked up. For good.

And the only way to accomplish that was with evidence.

The weather was relatively clear, though the wind had picked up a little. It wasn't bad yet, though occasionally a gust would catch him by surprise, reminding him how very little he knew about what he was doing. So much could go wrong, so easily.

The stark orange wooden stockade-style fence that surrounded Bruce Bromley's place peeked at them through the trees as they glided silently on the breeze toward the farm he'd visited only a few months before. Cutch realized his appraisal of the man's property had likely sparked Bruce's anger toward him. He'd appraised the property at a much higher value than it had been at previously, which would raise the man's property taxes significantly, but then, Bruce had made so many improvements to the land that Cutch's assessment had been completely fair.

On top of that, Bruce had surely recognized that Cutch's history would make him a good candidate if he ever needed someone to pin the meth production on. And since his pecan grove offered such a perfect place to hide, it had likely been too tempting a location for him to ignore. Any anger Bruce felt toward him for the raised tax rate would have easily sparked the kind of vengeful feelings that would lead him to move forward with his evil plan.

Cutch felt furious that the Bromleys would do such a

thing—even more so when he considered how close they were to getting away with it.

"Let's head for the northeast corner of the section," Cutch shouted to Elise as they neared Bruce's property. "The tree cover over there will block us from being seen by anyone in the main buildings."

"Okay, but don't try to fly too low. The last thing we want is to risk getting tangled in the trees."

"Sure thing," Cutch agreed. As they swept in over the property, Cutch scoured the area for any sign of a drug lab, praying that Bruce had chosen to keep his activities outside. If he hid the lab inside a building, there would be little evidence they could gather from the air. He swept along the tree line and tried to recall everything he could about the property from his earlier inspection.

Where would be a good place to hide a meth lab? Far away from the main house, that was for sure. Meth labs were dangerous—not just because of the toxic materials involved but because the volatile substances could easily explode. If Bruce was smart, he wouldn't keep them anywhere near his extravagant house.

As they flew low along the farthest reaches of the property, Cutch spotted something white near an old barn off to his left. An anhydrous tank? It sure looked like it. "I'm going to turn on my camera," he called to Elise. "Save yours for now."

When she nodded, he switched on the power, aiming his glider toward the tank he'd seen. He swept across the area, his gut knotting when he saw "Anhydrous Ammonia" on the side of the tank. Glad as he was to finally capture some evidence, he still hated having his worst assumptions confirmed. How many toxic drugs had the Bromley brothers poured into innocent Holyoake County? Far, far too many.

He circled wide, keeping his camera pointed at the spot.

"Camping fuel tanks," Elise called as she soared over a ravine that cut through the land. "I'm going to get some shots of this."

"Good." Cutch praised her efforts, though he felt even more disgusted with Bruce at her discovery. The ravine held a seasonal stream that fed into the Nishnabotna River and ultimately, the drinking water supplies of many communities downstream. And the Bromleys were disposing of their drugmaking waste there? They truly didn't care about anyone but themselves, did they?

"I think I've got enough pictures," Cutch called as the camera mounted on his speed bar stopped flashing. "Let's get out of here."

"I'm right on your tail," Elise called out over the sound of barking dogs.

Cutch looked back and saw a pair of Dobermans straining at their chains, barking. And not far behind them, he saw armed men leaping into SUVs.

They'd been spotted.

FOURTEEN

"Let's get out of here fast," Elise called to Cutch. She was pretty sure he'd seen the armed men climb into the SUVs that were peeling out in the direction of the wide archway that framed the main entrance to the Bromley estate, but she wanted to be sure he was headed away in the same direction she was. They'd already taken enough chances.

"I'm right behind you," Cutch called out. "Let's head north. If we can get above the hills that ought to slow them down, and the trees will give us some cover."

"Right," Elise agreed, though she felt a nauseating fear grab her. They were headed for the Loess Hills— where she'd been shot down once before by these guys. She knew from experience they wouldn't be safe there, but she couldn't think of a better option. And since the wind would push them faster in that direction, anyway, she figured it was the best shot they had at escaping.

Glancing behind them, she saw two black SUVs and a red truck raising dust as they sped along the gravel road after them. Elise steered toward the center of the fields. She'd still have to cross over every intersecting road, but she wasn't going to make herself an easier target than she already was.

"I sure wish we had a way of letting your dad know where we are," Cutch called out. "If he can get in touch with the DEA agents, maybe they can intercept these guys."

"I have my cell phone in my pocket," Elise shouted back over the wind. "Too bad I can't use it while I'm flying."

"Don't try it," Cutch yelled back. "It's too risky."

"Okay, but what else can we do?" She looked back. The trucks were gaining on them. More frightening still, she saw Darrel Stillwater's upper body sticking up from the passenger's window of the lead truck. He had a rifle on his shoulder, taking aim.

"They're closing in," she screeched, bracing herself and trying to angle her glider up to attain maximum elevation. She doubted she could fly out of their range entirely, but she could at least put some distance between them.

"Are there any sort of evasive maneuvers we can try?" Cutch asked.

"Not without slowing ourselves down." She looked out across the landscape, trying to find a place to hide or to lose their pursuers. The roads spread out at one-mile intervals in a perfect grid. They'd never be able to get more than a mile away from them, not unless they could find something—

"The river!" Cutch's shout interrupted her thoughts. "There's a bridge right up here, but if we can get a few miles past there, then fly across, they won't be able to reach us without driving several miles out of their way to the bridge. By then we could be long gone."

"Okay," Elise said in a shaking voice as she heard the pop of gunfire below them. "We just have to make it that far for your plan to work."

"Don't get too close yet or they might guess what we're up to," Cutch cautioned her.

"Right," Elise called back, not at all certain they could accomplish what he suggested. Another pop of gunfire from below was followed by a tearing sound. They'd hit her right wing.

"Elise!"

"It's just my wing," Elise assured Cutch, her heart warmed by the concern in his voice. "That won't slow me down too much."

In spite of her optimistic words, she felt the lightweight craft respond to the tear by refusing to push forward so quickly. Cutch passed her as her glider sagged behind.

"Come on! Hurry!" he called back.

She watched him swerve in the sky as though to circle back for her. "Keep going!" she insisted. "Don't put yourself at risk on my account."

As they passed over the center of the next section, she gulped a deep breath. They were as far away from the gunmen as they could get—for now. But they were quickly coming up on the next crossroad. And Bromley's men knew it.

Elise started praying more fervently. Up ahead of her, Cutch crossed over the road well ahead of the trucks. But as she approached the same spot, the pickup and SUVs came tearing along the road to meet her.

"Please God, *please*." She already knew Darrel had her within range, and she was fairly certain he was a pretty decent shot. She could only hope the dust clouds thrown up by their tires would cloud his vision enough for her to sneak past.

Blam!

Blam!

"Elise!" Cutch screamed.

Pain speared deep into the flesh above her right knee just as the motor behind her gasped and died. She was hit.

She was going down, and she wouldn't even be able to run away. This was it, then.

"Keep going. I'm okay!" Elise shouted for Cutch's benefit, though she felt far from okay. Cutch had to get away with the pictures they'd taken or they'd both be killed. She gripped the speed bar and bit back a scream as pain radiated up from the wound near her knee.

Cool air coming up off the river valley hit her face, lifting her torn glider. The Nishnabotna River paved its muddy track off to her right. If she tried to cross it, she could end up crashing into the middle of the river and be swept away in its swirling waters long before she could get her harness unhooked.

But if she stayed her course, she'd crash within a quarter mile of the men who'd shot her. And unless they changed their tactics, she'd be dead before she hit the ground. She turned toward the river, praying like crazy the lift off the water would be enough to carry her across and praying even harder that by some miracle she could then get away before the gunmen made it to the bridge and back.

She braced herself against the speed bar and angled her wounded glider for maximum lift. She could smell the muddy waters swirling below as she dipped close to the nearest bank.

The water gurgled, its thick late-summer stream deep and wide, nourished by the recent rains they'd received, and potentially deadly if she didn't make it across.

The roar of a motor behind her caught her attention, and she looked back. Though the red truck and one SUV were headed south toward the bridge three miles back, the third vehicle plowed through the fence rails that rimmed the field alongside the river, knocking them aside like sticks. The big beast of an SUV barreled straight toward her.

He was going to try to ford the river!

Elise glanced forward and saw Cutch circling back toward her. "Stay away!" she shouted, not wanting him to come within range of the gunman who was gaining on her in spite of the uneven, soggy ground along the river's banks.

She was halfway across the Nishnabotna but dropping steadily. Fortunately, the river was high, making the far bank a low one—which meant she had a shot of making it over but so did the SUV behind her.

With a splash, the vehicle hit the muddy water at high speed. It revved and rumbled for a few feet, throwing up water and mud, but it quickly settled in the deep, swirling waters. With a sickening sloshing sound, the submerged engine died. Cursing, the men crawled out the windows and up onto the roof, penned in by the swift current and the wide river.

The bank passed by underneath her. Elise tried to pull her legs up as her shoes skirted a bean field on the far side of the river. She screamed in pain as her wounded leg protested the movement. Though standard landing procedure required her to run along until she'd slowed the speed of the glider to a stop, she couldn't make her injured leg obey. She hopped on her good leg for a couple of strides and then gritted her teeth and landed hard, slumping down to her left and gasping for breath.

Moving fast, a plan already half-formed in her mind, she pulled the camera loose from its fresh tape and tied the tape like a tourniquet above her injury. Cutch might not have needed anything for his arm that morning, but his wound had only been superficial. Even without looking, she knew the bullet had penetrated deep into the muscle of her leg. To her relief, it looked like a clean shot that had missed the major veins, but that didn't mean she'd be able to use her leg. She'd need medical attention soon.

Unzipping her jacket pocket, she swapped the camera for her phone and hit the speed dial for her dad.

"Elise?" he answered immediately.

"I'm down by the Nishnabotna. East side, three miles north of the Shenandoah Bridge." She panted. "Did you get in touch with the DEA again?"

"They're on their way."

"Good. I have to go." She didn't wait for his response but closed the call before zipping the phone safely inside her pocket. She watched as Cutch landed his glider forty feet from her.

"No!" she shouted at him. "Take off, take off! You've got to get those pictures to the DEA. Dad got in touch with them. They're on their way."

"They're not going to get here before Bruce and his men. They're at the bridge now. We've got less than three minutes." As he spoke, Cutch unhooked himself from his harness and ran to her, reaching past her to the clasps that secured her harness to her glider.

"What are you doing?" she tried to push him away but grimaced as he brushed against her wounded leg.

"Elise?" He looked at her with concern, then followed her gaze down to where she'd tied the tape above the blood-soaked wound in her leg. "You're hit?"

"Yes." She bit back a sob and pushed him back. "Now leave. Get those pictures to the authorities. *Please,*" she pleaded with him.

But instead of obediently running for his glider, Cutch bent and scooped her up. "I'm not leaving you. We're down to two minutes." He ran with her to his glider and clipped her harness in place next to his before harnessing himself back to the glider.

"No," she protested as he prepared to take off. "It won't work, Cutch. We're too heavy. I can't run on this leg. We'll never get off the ground."

"Don't run," he said softly, his lips near her ear as he wrapped his arms around her. "Just hold the speed bar. I'll carry you."

Though she knew what he was trying to accomplish was likely impossible, Elise melted at the feel of Cutch's arms around her. She obediently grabbed the speed bar and gave a gasp as his strong arms lifted her feet off the ground just as he began to run down the field. She knew he'd been a standout on the track team years before, and obviously he was still in excellent shape, but she still doubted he could get up enough speed to get them both off the ground.

Still, she tried to tuck her legs up out of his way. The wound above her knee throbbed, but the tourniquet had cut off much of the feeling along with the flow of blood. Her lower leg felt heavy but otherwise mostly numb.

Cutch's long legs powered through a wide row in the bean field as the strong wings of the high-end glider caught the updraft coming off the river. The gusting wind billowed behind them, and Elise gripped the speed bar more tightly, as though she actually expected Cutch's foolish idea to work.

Over the sound of the powered glider's motor, she could hear the roar of the trucks coming up the road nearby to the east, but Cutch ran the length of the field alongside the river, keeping them the field's-width away from their pursuers. He seemed to gather speed even as the updraft lifted them off the ground.

"You did it!" she shrieked as they gained altitude.

"We did it." His words surprised her with their gentleness and closeness, and she felt her heart thumping from more than just fear. Cutch's arms wrapped around her securely, and she began to hope they might actually escape as they rose on the updraft that came up the riverside.

"Let's get back across the river. They'll have to go back to the bridge. That will buy us some time." Cutch whispered close to her, and she angled them in the direction he'd indicated, surprised to find they were able to manage the delicate steering with remarkable ease, even with her wounded leg. They just seemed to work well together.

They rose higher in the sky as they crossed the river and soon found themselves flying at a comfortable altitude. Elise allowed her tense body to relax slightly.

Cutch obviously noticed. "Don't worry. I've got you," he assured her in a soothing tone. "How's the leg?"

"Numb. Throbbing." A little shudder ran through her. "I don't want to think about it."

"Sorry."

"No, it's okay," she offered quickly. "I just don't want to think about how close I came…" She let her voice break off, certain he knew what she meant.

His arms tightened around her. "I was so scared for you. So scared. And for a moment I felt so helpless."

"I can't believe you came back for me. You could have gotten yourself killed, too."

His lips brushed against her ear in spite of their flying helmets. "I would do anything for you."

Elise couldn't suppress the little shiver that traveled through her, though she knew Cutch had to be aware of it. His words held so much promise, and she wondered what his earlier revelation meant. If he really felt so bad about embarrassing her that night eight years before, did that mean he really cared? Before she could allow her thoughts to drift too far, she needed to get to safety and get some medical attention for her leg.

"We've got to find a safe place to land," she reminded Cutch.

"How about the airfield? If your uncle Leroy is still there, he can help you with your leg."

The airfield wasn't far. "Good idea," she agreed. "But I don't know if he's still there. Bruce's men aren't that far behind us, either." She wished there was a way to contact the DEA agents and ask them to meet them at the airfield.

Maybe there was.

"Can you take the speed bar?" she asked.

"I don't want to let go of you."

"I'm harnessed in. I won't fall. But somebody needs to steer this thing with both hands."

"What are you going to do?"

"I'm going to try to call Leroy."

Cutch hesitated. "Okay," he agreed slowly and loosened the hold he had on her. When it was clear the harness mechanism secured her safely to the glider, Cutch let go and placed his hands next to hers on the speed bar.

"Got it?" she asked.

"Got it."

Elise let go, well aware that she was placing all her trust—and her life—in Cutch's hands. She quickly pulled the phone from her zippered pocket, careful not to drop it into the fields and trees below them, and zipped the pocket closed again over the camera that was still inside. She hit the speed dial for her uncle's phone.

"Hello?" Leroy answered the phone with concern in his voice.

"It's Elise. Are you at the airfield?"

"I am." Leroy cleared his throat. "The sheriff is here—Sheriff Bromley. He's waiting," Leroy dropped his voice, and Elise could just imagine the sheriff standing by,

watching him and listening in. "Don't come," Leroy whispered, his words sputtering out with a cough.

His message carried through loud and clear.

Elise thanked him and snapped the phone shut, relieved that she'd found out before sailing right into the sheriff's trap.

"Did Leroy just say the sheriff is there?" Cutch asked, having likely overheard the whole conversation.

"Yes." Elise bit back the fear that threatened to overwhelm her voice. When she looked back, she could see the red pickup truck and the last black SUV had already crossed the bridge again and were now tearing up the road, gaining on them. "Now where are we going to go? We need someplace to land—someplace close. Someplace we can hide but where the Feds can meet us."

"The Old McCutcheon airstrip," Cutch suggested.

"What?" Elise didn't realize the place still existed. "Where's that?"

"Back across the river. It's overgrown, but the buildings are still there. Grandpa Scarth bought it from Grandpa McCutcheon years ago, pretty much as a favor to him when his money ran low. Grandpa's never done a thing with it. But the old airstrip isn't too overrun, and there are plenty of buildings to hide in. Call your dad. Tell him to meet us out there and to bring the DEA agents."

"Will my father know where it is?"

"I'm sure he does," Cutch said. "Just ask him."

Elise got back on the phone.

Her father sounded relieved to hear her voice. "Where are you?" he asked.

"We're in the sky, headed toward the old McCutcheon airstrip. Do you know where that is?"

"Of course I do."

The pop of a gun behind them caused Elise to look back. Bromley and his men were within shooting range.

"Try to meet us there. Bring help—the DEA and paramedics. I have to go." Elise hurried to put the phone in her pocket, zipping it shut tight before placing her hands next to Cutch's on the speed bar. She'd need to focus if they were going to steer the glider back across the river. It was their only hope for staying ahead of Bruce Bromley and his men.

"Ready?" Cutch asked, and she could feel him tensing in preparation for the turn.

"Ready," she agreed with a slight nod, and they angled their bodies as they pointed the nose of the glider back toward the Nishnabotna. Once again, she was amazed and pleased at how well they worked together. They swept over the swirling waters, and Cutch helped her guide the craft in the direction of the old McCutcheon airstrip.

Elise looked down behind them to check on Bruce and his men. "They're splitting up," she informed Cutch. "The red truck is heading north, and the black SUV is going south."

"Makes sense. They don't know which way we're going to go once we get across, and we're about halfway between the Shenandoah and Essex Bridges. So either way, one of them will be able to catch us in a hurry."

"And tell Sheriff Bromley where to find us," Elise finished for him. "We won't have much of a lead. I just hope Dad gets there soon."

"And I hope the Feds are with him. Did he say where they're coming from?"

"I have no idea." Elise hated to admit it. "He said the DEA was sending people, but unless they're coming from nearby, it could be an hour or even several hours before they get here. And if Bruce tells his brother where we're headed, he'll get there first." Her fear nearly choked off her words, but she felt the comforting touch of Cutch's arms, as he let go of the speed bar she held and wrapped his arms around her again. She let herself relax a little in his arms. She didn't have much choice. The pain of the injury to her leg made her feel lightheaded.

"We're not going down without a fight," he whispered. "God has brought us this far."

Elise gulped a strengthening breath. "Whatever happens, we have to make sure the pictures make it to the authorities. Bruce Bromley's drug operation has to be stopped."

FIFTEEN

Cutch saw the dilapidated McCutcheon airstrip come into view. He reluctantly let go of Elise and took hold of the speed bar with resignation. They had to make it there if they were going to survive. But once they did, he'd no longer have any excuse to hold Elise in his arms. For a moment, he wished their desperate flight through the sky would last forever.

But the strain of their combined weight was already taking its toll on the glider, and he didn't have to do much to get them pointed down toward the old landing strip. The ground came up to meet them quickly, and Cutch told Elise, "Keep your legs up. I'll land us."

He tried to avoid jostling her wounded leg, but he still saw the look of pain that shot across her features as they came to a stop and he grabbed her arms to steady her. She looked pale.

"You hanging in there?" he asked as he unclipped her harness and grabbed her up into his arms as gently as he could.

"Mmm-hmm." She slumped against him without even putting up a fight.

Not a good sign.

With Elise in his arms, Cutch ran for the rundown hangar, peeling back a rusty section of tin siding far enough to permit them to duck in, since the doors were held shut with padlocks. It had been years since he and his little sister, Ginny, had played hide-and-seek there on trips with their grandfather, and for the first time he was glad the place had never been fixed up. All his old hiding places should still be around.

Pulling the tin back into place after them, Cutch hurried through the dim building to one of his favorite hiding places in the cockpit of a long-dead biplane that had been parked there for longer than he'd been alive. Years ago, his grandpa McCutcheon had tried to get the old bird to fly, but just like his pecan groves, he'd never been able to make her go.

And his grandpa Scarth had held onto the plane out of nostalgia and respect for the dead. It had been the only plane out of his grandpa McCutcheon's fleet that hadn't been sold off over the years to pay the bills. Cutch hoisted Elise up into the little two-seater, and the old leather seats creaked with age beneath them as they settled in. As he looked at the gleaming control panel before him, however, Cutch realized the plane had seen some attention as of late.

"I think I know what Grandpa Scarth has been working on so secretively," he observed. As his eyes adjusted to the dim light inside the dusty building, he realized the plane had been completely redone. He wondered if his grandpa had finally gotten it to the point where it would fly again. It seemed unlikely since the plane was so old. More than likely the improvements were merely cosmetic.

Elise looked up at him with shadowed eyes and asked in a drained voice, "Is this our hiding place?"

"Sure is." Cutch settled into place beside her as she slumped heavily against his shoulder. Also not a good sign. "This old plane was built to withstand enemy fire. It's as good a hiding place as any and safer than most." The large hangar was full of old junk, besides the junk-filled outbuildings. Bromley and his men would have plenty of places to look for them—unless they thought to check the plane first.

He thought he heard a vehicle approaching outside, and he felt Elise tense slightly. She'd obviously heard it, too, though her shallow breathing told him she was no longer as alert as she'd been. She'd lost a lot of blood. He wondered how much longer she'd be able to hang in there. While he listened to the activity outside, he prayed the paramedics would reach them before Elise suffered much more.

Outside, the engine stilled and doors slammed. Cutch could hear indistinct shouting and in the distance, sirens. He hoped the paramedics were on their way, or even the federal authorities, but he feared it might be Gideon Bromley and his deputies using the long arm of the law to protect his brother's drug ring.

He shifted Elise against his shoulder and tried to make her comfortable. "Elise, honey, hang in there. Help is on the way. It won't be much longer." He prayed the words were true.

Her weak hands clung to the fabric of his shirt as she leaned against him.

She'd given it her all. Cutch could hardly believe what she'd endured that day—and all for his sake. She could have walked away and let him rot in jail, but instead, she'd come to his aid and flown at his side. His heart swelled inside him.

"I love you so much." The words escaped from his mouth before he realized he'd consciously thought them.

Elise's eyes opened, and she seemed to regain some of her strength as she looked up at him. "You what?"

Realizing the words were true and hoping hearing them again would distract her from her injury, Cutch repeated, "I love you, Elise. I'm sorry I let you down. If there was anything I could do to make it up to you, I'd do it in a heartbeat."

Before he could continue, the muffled noises outside burst into sharp clarity as Darrel's deep voice shouted, "Come out, or we'll burn down every building here. We know you're in there. Come out before we light this place on fire!"

Fear replaced the pain on Elise's face. Cutch let out a long breath and frantically tried to think. The old wood-and-tin building would burn like so many matchsticks, its dusty contents nothing more than tinder to fuel the flames. If Bromley's men decided to torch the place, he and Elise would be done for. In a way, he figured he was lucky the man had given them a choice.

He doubted the window of opportunity would be open for long.

He shifted Elise gently away from his shoulder. "I'm going out there."

Elise gripped the front of Cutch's shirt tightly, as though she could hold him back with the feeble strength of her weakening hands. "No," she whispered.

"I've got to. If they light a match, we're dead."

"The Feds are on their way," Elise reminded him. "And my dad."

"Unless they've got a fire brigade with them, they're

not going to be able to stop Bromley. This might be my only chance. If I go out there now, I might be able to stall them until help arrives."

"Cutch," she pleaded, refusing to let go of his shirt. "They'll shoot you."

He froze. The seconds ticked by while the men outside issued another gruff warning. A bright orange flash of light flared beyond one of the dusty old windows, and Elise realized the men had torched one of the outbuildings. They were trying to flush them out.

"I need to hurry," he said, pulling away from her as the angry shouts escalated outside.

"Don't leave me." Elise tried to grab hold of his shirt again, but he was already climbing out of the plane. She wasn't sure exactly what the men outside had planned, but she felt certain if Cutch turned himself over that they'd kill him.

Not that their odds were very good if they stayed inside the building, either. "Cutch," she called after him, wishing her voice was stronger but unable to muster up any more volume in her weakened state. She couldn't let him leave without telling him how she truly felt—not if he was going out to his death. "I love you."

His eyes level with the cockpit as he climbed down, Cutch froze and met her eyes. "What?" he asked, surprise and hope filling his face.

Elise bit back the pain that speared through her leg and leaned toward him. "I love you. I don't want to love you. I tried not to. I didn't want to get hurt again," she started to explain, but Cutch hoisted himself back into the cockpit and wrapped his arms gently around her.

"Can I kiss you?" he asked, his lips mere inches from hers.

"I've always wanted you to, but the last time—" her voice caught.

His nose brushed hers, as he whispered, "This won't be anything like our last kiss. I know how much you mean to me now."

Just as his lips were about to meet hers, she heard a ruckus outside. Cutch pulled back, his expression intent as they both listened to sort out what was going on.

Shouting met shouting. Uncle Leroy's bellowing voice was easy to identify—he was the one threatening to shoot the next person who moved. Grandpa Scarth's voice didn't sound so old as he accused Bromley and his men of trespassing on private property. The lone female voice was clearly Anita McCutcheon. She hollered, "You'll have to go through me first!"

And the calmer men's voices that tried to reason with everyone had to belong to their fathers. As Elise squinted through the dusty windows at the front end of the hangar, she could see her father and Old Cutch standing side by side.

Cutch squeezed her hand gently. "They're uniting to protect us."

A lump filled Elise's throat. Eight years before, she'd prayed every night that their families would get over the feud that ran between them. God had finally answered her prayer.

But a moment later, she wondered if they hadn't come too late. A loud whooshing noise filled the room as the back end of the dilapidated hangar burst into flames.

The building was on fire.

Cutch quickly assessed their situation. The entire back end of the building was on fire, and the flames were quickly spreading to the dry contents and along the side walls. Bruce and his men had likely doused the building with gasoline. The fire burned quickly and smoke began to fill the air.

Elise clung to him. "We've got to get out of here."

"I know." Cutch looked back toward the place where they'd come in. Just as he began to wonder if they had any chance of sneaking out that way, flames ignited all along the back wall. He didn't know how Bruce's men had managed to sneak past all their relatives who'd come to their aid, but one thing was clear: Bruce Bromley wasn't playing around.

"There's no way out," Elise gasped. "We're surrounded by fire. What are we going to do?"

Cutch looked down and began to pray. He got no further than, "Lord, help us," when his eyes landed on the shiny key stuck in the plane's ignition. Had his Grandpa Scarth really fixed up the plane enough to make it fly? Or had his improvements been merely cosmetic? There was only one way to find out.

"Hold on tight," Cutch cautioned Elise as he reached for the key and gave it a turn. To his shock and relief, the motor revved smoothly.

"What are you doing?" Elise screeched. "Does this old plane really fly?"

"We're going to find out," Cutch said, looking for the throttle. "Help me figure out how to fly this thing."

"You've got to free the brake first," Elise reached past him and something popped. "Now rev it like you mean it."

While Elise worked the controls, Cutch turned the steering wheel and pointed them toward the wall that had been burning the longest. The old wood was probably burned nearly through. In fact, the roof would likely soon collapse. He was glad for the broad wings that shielded the cockpit. They'd need all the cover they could get.

The plane lurched forward under Elise's able hands and gathered speed as it plowed past the clutter between them and the burning wall. Cutch instinctively threw his hands up, covering their faces as they burst through the wall. He was glad the old war plane had been built to withstand enemy fire.

An instant later they were breezing down the runway along the open field. They could breathe again.

Elise coughed and slumped against him. "You fly," she said weakly.

Cutch realized she'd probably exhausted the last of her reserves of strength getting them out of the building. It had been years since Grandpa McCutcheon had given him flying lessons, but Cutch had watched Elise enough times over the last couple of days to recall the basics that his grandfather had insisted he learn all those years ago.

Glancing behind them, he saw Bruce and his men scrambling to get away from the building as the hole they'd made with the plane set off a domino effect that brought the rest of the roof down. Through the thick smoke that filled the sky, he spotted several more vehicles coming up the roads. More of Bromley's men? Or were they on his side? He couldn't see nearly enough to tell through the black smoke that filled the air, so he turned his attention back to getting the plane in the sky.

They skipped and bumped down the last of the runway before finally lifting off.

So his grandfather's old plane really could fly.

Cutch felt a warm sense of satisfaction coupled with the relief of escaping the enemy's hands. He wasn't sure how well the plane would fly, especially after plowing through the burning wall of the hangar, so he kept it fairly low in the sky and circled the airstrip, trying to make out what was going on below.

"You hanging in there?" he asked Elise as she clung weakly to his shoulders, her eyes closed.

"I'm fine."

Cutch would have laughed at her blatantly inaccurate prognosis if he hadn't been so concerned for her. "It looks like your uncle Leroy and your dad are both down there, along with some folks I don't recognize," Cutch updated her as he circled around for another pass. "As soon as I think it's safe, I'll land us."

"Are the paramedics there yet?"

"I think I see them pulling in."

"Good."

"Want to go down?"

"Do you think it's safe?"

"Somebody just slapped cuffs on Bruce Bromley," Cutch relayed, "and it looks like they're giving Gideon the what for." As he circled past the smoke, Cutch recognized more vehicles and people. "There's my dad talking to your dad."

With a final wide arc, Cutch aligned himself with the landing strip. "Let's go talk to them." He tried to speak casually, but his heart was in knots. He'd never thought he'd see the day when the two men would speak civilly to one another. Yet there they were.

Cutch brought the plane down as gently as he could, wishing he could spare Elise any more jostling than she'd already endured. He taxied the plane toward where his grandfather ran excitedly to meet them. Then he scooped Elise tenderly against him and disembarked.

"She flies, she flies," Grandpa Scarth hooted with delight, clapping his hands. "Surprise, surprise."

Old Cutch came up behind his father-in-law. "My dad's plane flies? I never thought…"

Grandpa Scarth clapped Old Cutch on the shoulders. "He always said she was a good plane. He was right."

Bill and Leroy McAlister hurried toward them. "Elise?" Bill asked, reaching them first. "Is she okay?"

"She should be fine." Cutch tried to placate Bill's fears as he carried Elise toward where an ambulance had come to a stop. "She was shot in the leg. She's lost a lot of blood."

The paramedics pulled out a gurney as he trotted over to them, and he lowered Elise carefully onto its waiting surface before tucking her hair back out of her eyes, behind her ears the way he knew she liked it. She blinked at him and gave him a weak smile before lying back and closing her eyes.

"She's probably going to need a blood transfusion," Cutch offered, showing the medics her injury and slipping the camera from where she'd kept it safely zipped away in her pocket.

He handed over both cameras to Leroy McAlister. "See that the authorities get these."

"Don't you want to talk to them?" Leroy asked.

Cutch shook his head and was about to explain when his father slumped down. Bill McAlister stepped to his side, supporting his weight.

"I'm okay. I'm okay," Old Cutch insisted, though he didn't look it.

The paramedics prepared to load Elise into the ambulance.

"I'd like to ride along," Cutch requested.

"But your father," Elise protested weakly.

Cutch looked back at his dad, who was standing again, though he leaned heavily on his one-time enemy. His dad waved him on. "You go," he mouthed silently.

Knowing he'd picked his father over Elise once before, Cutch climbed into the ambulance after her as soon as she was loaded in.

With a loud whoosh, the final wall of the burning hangar fell, and the ambulance took off with a wail from its sirens.

As Cutch had figured, Elise needed to be taken into surgery to have the wound in her leg repaired, but the procedure was nearly completed by the time the rest of their family members arrived at the hospital, and the doctor assured them she'd make a full recovery.

"You can take turns going into the recovery room one at a time. She'll be a little groggy at first, but she should be waking up soon."

Cutch met Bill McAlister's eyes.

"I suppose you want to be the first to go in there." Bill met his eyes with a look of challenge.

"I'd like to, but I understand if—"

"Hurry up, then. She'll be wondering where everyone went." Bill cut him off.

Cutch grinned and took two steps in the direction of the door before he stopped and said, "Thank you. And, sir? Could I marry your daughter?"

Elise's father froze and looked at him for a long minute. "I think that's up to her," he said finally.

"But I have your blessing?" Cutch pressed. After all the animosity their families had shared, he couldn't imagine beginning a life—and eventually a family—with Elise unless he knew they had their families' support and approval.

"You do," Bill pronounced, just as his brother Leroy joined in the conversation.

"But if you ever hurt her, you'll wish I'd have just shot you when you stole my ladder," Leroy threatened.

Cutch's laughter was only slightly nervous as he stepped into the recovery room.

Elise's eyelids fluttered open. "Cutch?"

"I hope you're not disappointed to see me."

"You're the person I was hoping to see." Her words came out like a sigh, and she coughed dryly.

"Would you like a drink of water?" he asked, reaching for her hospital mug and holding the straw for her to drink.

She took a long sip and smiled up at him.

His heart dipped. He couldn't wait any longer but leaned close to her and whispered, "Will you marry me?"

Elise looked up at Cutch and blinked. She was still in a bit of a fog and wasn't exactly sure what was going on. She'd had some very Cutch-filled dreams in the last couple of hours and wondered if she might still be stuck in one of them. Since she'd finally allowed herself to fall back in love with him, she'd begun to hope they might have a chance for a future together. But obviously it was far too soon to get too serious about the idea. She must be dreaming.

She shook her head a little and tried to remember what had been going on. "Did they catch the Bromleys?" she asked.

Cutch frowned. "Yes. And the Bromley brothers are acting like kids about it. Bruce is trying to blame the whole bit on Gideon, who claims he had no idea what his brother was up to. He insists he had nothing to do with the drugs or even with their plans to frame me. They're both behind bars for now, and Gideon has stepped down as sheriff pending a full investigation. For Gideon's sake, I hope he's right about being innocent. He always seemed like a good man to me."

"But you've been cleared of all charges?"

"Not officially, but I expect that will come soon. The Feds have already indicated as much. They've known for a long time that someone was producing meth in this county, and Bruce fits the profile of the information they'd gathered so far, besides all the materials they found on his land. They were very appreciative for our help in catching him."

"That's a relief." She looked up into his face, and her heart skipped a beat. His expression was so intense, his blue eyes unswerving as he looked at her. All the feelings she'd pushed away for the last eight years came rushing back, and she felt a little lightheaded. "Am I going to be okay?"

"Yes," Cutch assured her, reaching forward and brushing back a stray hair that had escaped from the tucking place behind her right ear. "Your leg muscles just need to heal. The bullet missed the bone and major vessels. They say you were really very fortunate."

Elise relaxed a little. "God was watching out for me,"

she said with assurance. When she glanced back up at Cutch, he looked a little concerned. Her heart went out to him. He'd done so much for her—risked so much to save her. She wondered if he realized how much she loved him. "Cutch—" she started, when a knock at the door interrupted her.

They both looked up as her father poked his head into the room.

"Well? What did she say?" he asked expectantly.

Cutch looked sheepish. "I, uh—"

"Haven't you asked her yet?" Leroy peeked over his brother's shoulder.

"I did, but she hasn't—" Cutch began.

Elise looked back and forth between them, wondering what was going on. She was still quite fuzzy from the anesthesia. They couldn't possibly mean...

A third head appeared in the doorway. "Are we awake? Time to take your vitals." A nurse brushed past the McAlister men and popped a thermometer under Elise's tongue. She squirmed, wanting desperately to ask what question she was supposed to be answering.

"Knock-knock!" Anita McCutcheon appeared in the doorway along with Cutch's Grandpa Scarth. She held a giant balloon bouquet. "I couldn't wait at home any longer," Anita announced. "Old Cutch has been sleeping like a baby since we got home, and I've been just about fit to burst waiting to find out what she said." Anita turned and looked at Elise with interest.

Elise looked at the crowd of people—McCutcheons and McAlisters all squeezed into the doorway together—and suddenly felt overwhelmed. When the nurse finally removed the thermometer from her mouth, she took a deep breath.

"You have too many visitors. The doctor said only one person in the room at a time," the nurse chirped, strapping a blood pressure cuff on her arm. She addressed Cutch, "You've had your turn. Out." She gestured with her head for him to leave.

"Just a second." Cutch ducked his head past the cuff and leaned close to Elise's ear. "Please?" he whispered.

Elise's heart fluttered as his nose brushed her skin. She wished everyone else would disappear so she could be alone with Cutch. But more than that, she wanted to know what question everyone was talking about. "I—I think I missed something," she admitted sheepishly.

A smile played across Cutch's lips. "Will you marry me?" he asked softly, nuzzling her cheek as he spoke.

Elise gave a tiny gasp. "You mean I didn't dream that part?" She reached her free arm around and cupped his cheek. "I've loved you for so long, Cutch. But I didn't think…" She looked back to the doorway at all the shining faces gazing down at her. All these people who'd kept them apart for so long had been brought together. Long ago she'd naively hoped the strength of her love for Cutch could overcome the feud.

And it finally had.

"Yes," she answered, her eyes shining. She could envision a happy wedding with both their families present. And her mother, who'd never wanted to leave her, could be a part of the celebration, too. "Yes, I'll marry you."

As Cutch leaned forward to plant the long-awaited kiss on her lips, the nurse snapped off the blood pressure cuff with a sigh.

"Okay, fine. He can stay, but the rest of you need to leave."

"I agree. They could use some privacy," Anita McCutcheon called over her shoulder as she walked back down the hall. "I'm just glad to see it all ended so well."

"Me, too," Bill McAlister agreed.

But Elise wasn't listening. She was finally kissing the man she loved.

* * * * *

Dear Reader,

Cutch and Elise's story makes me feel homesick for southwest Iowa and all the warmhearted people who live there. The Loess Hills are a real place, as is the Nishnabotna River, though Holyoake, Iowa, is a figment of my imagination, based loosely on my husband's hometown of Clarinda and its sister city, Shenandoah. Though Holyoake is fictional, it still feels like home.

Likewise, the characters in this story feel very real to me. Misunderstandings and hurt feelings caused a rift between the McCutcheons and the McAlisters—a rift that only God's love can ultimately overcome. Though the feud between them is a bitter one, it's rooted in honest, loving feelings, as one generation has tried to protect the next from suffering through the hurts and broken hearts that sometimes go along with life.

I hope you've enjoyed your visit to Holyoake County, and I pray you'll join me there again as some of the characters we've come to love find happy endings of their own. Please visit my website at www.rachellemccalla.com for recipes, character updates and exciting news about forthcoming stories.

God bless you, and thanks for reading this book!

Rachelle McCalla

QUESTIONS FOR DISCUSSION

1. As Elise's glider is shot down, she prays that God will help her escape from her enemies. Do you believe God answered her prayers? How?

2. Cutch is particularly distressed to discover someone has been producing meth on his property. Why does he feel so strongly about this issue? Have you ever felt more passionately about an issue because of personal experience or a loved one's experience?

3. Elise's father and Uncle Leroy are very protective of her. What are the advantages and disadvantages of their behavior? Have you ever felt someone was being overprotective toward you? Have you ever been overprotective toward someone else?

4. Though Cutch wants to investigate the tank he saw from the sky, he chooses to help Elise first, only to discover the tank has been moved while he was helping her. Have you ever felt you'd lost out on something important by helping a friend? How did you deal with your feelings? What did you ultimately gain through your sacrifice?

5. Cutch is a secretive person by nature and often gives Elise an evasive answer when she asks him a question, especially toward the start of their adventure. How is her ability to trust him influenced by his unwillingness to share? When he begins to open up, how does

Elise respond? Have you ever known someone who was secretive? How did their behavior impact your relationship with them?

6. Though Elise still feels strongly attracted to Cutch, she refuses to let on to him about her true feelings. Why? How is her silence helpful? How is it harmful?

7. Elise feels abandoned by her mother and thinks she's unlovable. Because of her mother's rejection, Elise feels certain Cutch will always reject her as well. Do her feelings make sense to you? Have you ever transferred a feeling—either rejection, criticism or approval from one person to another? How have these transferred emotions hindered your relationships? How can you overcome that?

8. When Pastor Carmichael preaches about loving enemies, Elise listens to his message while coming up with excuses in her mind for why she shouldn't do what the Bible says. Have you ever done something similar? Was Elise best served by following her ideas of what was right or by following the Bible's instructions? What is God calling you to do?

9. Cutch's grandfather planted his pecan trees too close together for them to be fruitful. Though Cutch has pruned them to make them more productive, they'll never yield what they could have if they'd been correctly planted initially. How are our lives like the pecan trees? What decisions have you made that have made your life less fruitful? What have you had to prune? Can you think of any Bible passages that relate our lives to bearing trees?

10. Cutch reflects on the Bible's promise that the truth will set a person free. He fears the sheriff's investigation will do the opposite for him. In what ways are his fears realized? In what ways does the whole truth finally set him free? Have you ever found yourself waiting for the whole truth to set you free? What does that promise from the Bible really mean (see John 8:32; 14.6)?

11. When Elise revisits the Bible passage from Luke 6:27-31, she realizes God calls her to love, even if she isn't loved in return. How does this realization change Elise's attitude toward Cutch? How does it free her from her fears? Is there someone difficult in your life who God is calling you to love?

12. When Elise's father explains the history between the feuding families, Elise realizes much of her anger toward Cutch was brought on by things that had happened long ago—in some cases, before she was even born. How do things that happened long ago influence the way you treat others? Can you think of historical or biblical examples of this dynamic? What long-held grudges can you overcome today?

13. Both the McCutcheons and McAlisters are God-loving people who are active in church, who pray and read their Bibles regularly. Yet they still maintain an ugly feud that generates bitterness and hatred between their families. Do you think this is believable? How does it challenge the assumption that Christians are supposed to lead perfect lives? Is there any ugliness in your heart that you need to confess and be forgiven for

today? How does this make you feel more sympathetic toward other "hypocritical" Christians?

14. Given all the evidence that's stacked against Cutch, Elise feels like she's going out on a limb to trust him. Do you think her decisions were wise? What might you have done differently?

15. Throughout the book, Cutch and Elise often note that God has been watching out for them, helping them to escape from the bad guys, no matter how close they've come to getting caught. How does this correspond with your own experience of God's protection? What can you do today to trust Christ more?

Love Inspired ®
SUSPENSE

TITLES AVAILABLE NEXT MONTH

Available October 12, 2010

CRITICAL IMPACT
Whisper Lake
Linda Hall

INTO THE DEEP
Virginia Smith

BETRAYAL IN THE BADLANDS
Dana Mentink

UNDER THE MARSHAL'S PROTECTION
Kathleen Tailer

LARGER-PRINT BOOKS!

**GET 2 FREE
LARGER-PRINT NOVELS
PLUS 2 FREE
MYSTERY GIFTS**

Love Inspired®

SUSPENSE

RIVETING INSPIRATIONAL ROMANCE

Larger-print novels are now available...

YES! Please send me 2 FREE LARGER-PRINT Love Inspired® Suspense novels and my 2 FREE mystery gifts (gifts are worth about $10). After receiving them, if I don't wish to receive any more books, I can return the shipping statement marked "cancel". If I don't cancel, I will receive 4 brand-new novels every month and be billed just $4.74 per book in the U.S. or $5.24 per book in Canada. That's a saving of over 20% off the cover price. It's quite a bargain! Shipping and handling is just 50¢ per book.* I understand that accepting the 2 free books and gifts places me under no obligation to buy anything. I can always return a shipment and cancel at any time. Even if I never buy another book, the two free books and gifts are mine to keep forever.

110/310 IDN E7RD

Name _____ (PLEASE PRINT)

Address _____ Apt. #

City _____ State/Prov. _____ Zip/Postal Code

Signature (if under 18, a parent or guardian must sign)

Mail to **Steeple Hill Reader Service:**
IN U.S.A.: P.O. Box 1867, Buffalo, NY 14240-1867
IN CANADA: P.O. Box 609, Fort Erie, Ontario L2A 5X3
Not valid for current subscribers to Love Inspired Suspense larger-print books.

**Are you a current subscriber to Love Inspired Suspense books
and want to receive the larger-print edition?
Call 1-800-873-8635 or visit www.morefreebooks.com.**

* Terms and prices subject to change without notice. Prices do not include applicable taxes. Sales tax applicable in N.Y. Canadian residents will be charged applicable provincial taxes and GST. Offer not valid in Quebec. This offer is limited to one order per household. All orders subject to approval. Credit or debit balances in a customer's account(s) may be offset by any other outstanding balance owed by or to the customer. Please allow 4 to 6 weeks for delivery. Offer available while quantities last.

Your Privacy: Steeple Hill Books is committed to protecting your privacy. Our Privacy Policy is available online at www.SteepleHill.com or upon request from the Reader Service. From time to time we make our lists of customers available to reputable third parties who may have a product or service of interest to you. If you would prefer we not share your name and address, please check here. ☐

Help us get it right—We strive for accurate, respectful and relevant communications. To clarify or modify your communication preferences, visit us at www.ReaderService.com/consumerschoice.

LISUSLP10R

HARLEQUIN®

A Romance

FOR EVERY MOOD™

Spotlight on

Inspirational

Wholesome romances
that touch the heart and soul.

See the next page
to enjoy a sneak peek from
the Love Inspired® inspirational series.

*See below for a sneak peek at
our inspirational line, Love Inspired®.
Introducing HIS HOLIDAY BRIDE
by bestselling author Jillian Hart*

Autumn Granger gave her horse rein to slide toward the town's new sheriff.

"Hey, there." The man in a brand-new Stetson, black T-shirt, jeans and riding boots held up a hand in greeting. He stepped away from his four-wheel drive with "Sheriff" in black on the doors and waded through the grasses. "I'm new around here."

"I'm Autumn Granger."

"Nice to meet you, Miss Granger. I'm Ford Sherman, from Chicago." He knuckled back his hat, revealing the most handsome face she'd ever seen. Big blue eyes contrasted with his sun-tanned complexion.

"I'm guessing you haven't seen much open land. Out here, you've got to keep an eye on cows or they're going to tear your vehicle apart."

"What?" He whipped around. Sure enough, mammoth black-and-white creatures had started to gnaw on his four-wheel drive. They clustered like a mob, mouths and tongues and teeth bent on destruction. One cow tried to pry the wiper off the windshield, another chewed on the side mirror. Several leaned through the open window, licking the seats.

"Move along, little dogie." He didn't know the first thing about cattle.

The entire herd swiveled their heads to study him curiously. Not a single hoof shifted. The animals soon returned to chewing, licking, digging through his possessions.

Autumn laughed, a warm and wonderful sound. "Thanks,

I needed that." She then pulled a bag from behind her saddle and waved it at the cows. "Look what I have, guys. Cookies."

Cows swung in her direction, and dozens of liquid brown eyes brightened with cookie hopes. As she circled the car, the cattle bounded after her. The earth shook with the force of their powerful hooves.

"Next time, you're on your own, city boy." She tipped her hat. The cowgirl stayed on his mind, the sweetest thing he had ever seen.

*Will Ford be able to stick it out in the country
to find out more about Autumn?
Find out in HIS HOLIDAY BRIDE
by bestselling author Jillian Hart,
available in October 2010
only from Love Inspired®.*